永恆的莎士比亞改寫劇本 ❼

威尼斯商人

THE MERCHANT OF VENICE

William Shakespeare ◆ 著

Emily Hutchinson ◆ 改寫　　蔡裴驊 ◆ 譯

MP3

永恆的莎士比亞改寫劇本 ❼
威尼斯商人
THE MERCHANT OF VENICE

作　　者	William Shakespeare, Emily Hutchinson
翻　　譯	蔡裴騏
編　　輯	Gina Wang
校　　對	丁宥榆
內文排版	林書玉
封面設計	林書玉
製程管理	洪巧玲
出 版 者	寂天文化事業股份有限公司
電　　話	+886-(0)2-2365-9739
傳　　真	+886-(0)2-2365-9835
網　　址	www.icosmos.com.tw
讀者服務	onlineservice@icosmos.com.tw
出版日期	2016 年 9 月 初版一刷

版權所有 請勿翻印
郵撥帳號 1998620-0 寂天文化事業股份有限公司
劃撥金額 600（含）元以上者，郵資免費。
訂購金額 600 元以下者，加收 65 元運費。
〔若有破損，請寄回更換，謝謝〕

國家圖書館出版品預行編目 (CIP) 資料

永恆的莎士比亞改寫劇本 .7：威尼斯商人 / William
Shakespeare, Emily Hutchinson 作；蔡裴騏譯 . -- 初版 .
-- [臺北市]：寂天文化，2016.09
　面；　公分
ISBN 978-986-318-500-0(平裝附光碟片)

873.43341　　　　　　　　　　　　　　105016820

Contents

Background 🎧

Bassanio asks his friend Antonio for money to woo the heiress Portia. Antonio borrows the money from Shylock, a Jewish moneylender. Because Shylock hates all Christians—and Antonio in particular—he foregoes his usual interest. Instead, he asks for a pound of Antonio's flesh if the money is not repaid in three months.

Then Antonio's business goes bad. He loses all his money and is unable to repay Shylock. Now even angrier toward Christians because of his daughter's elopement with one, Shylock wants his pound of flesh. All looks hopeless until Portia shows up at the trial, dressed as a judge. Will she be clever enough to render a fair judgment and thus save poor Antonio's life?

—— Cast of Characters  ——

THE DUKE OF VENICE, PRINCE OF MOROCCO,
    and PRINCE OF ARAGON: Suitors to Portia

ANTONIO: A merchant of Venice

BASSANIO: Antonio's friend

GRATIANO, SOLANIO, and SALERIO: Friends of
    Antonio and Bassanio

LORENZO: In love with Jessica

SHYLOCK: A Jewish moneylender

TUBAL: Another Jew, and friend of Shylock

LANCELOT GOBBO: Servant to Shylock and later Bassanio

OLD GOBBO: Lancelot's father

LEONARDO: Servant to Bassanio

BALTHAZAR and STEPHANO: Servants to Portia

PORTIA: A wealthy lady of Belmont

NERISSA: Portia's waiting-maid

JESSICA: Shylock's daughter

OFFICERS OF THE COURT OF JUSTICE, A JAILER, SERVANTS,
    AND ATTENDANTS

ACT 1

Summary

安東尼歐與他的朋友撒萊利歐和索拉尼歐談及他難過的心情，他的朋友們試圖鼓舞他，使他開心，而巴薩尼歐也與其他兩位朋友前來。當其他人離開時，巴薩尼歐向安東尼歐借錢，因他想去貝爾蒙追求一位富有的女繼承人。安東尼歐表示他手頭很緊，但他會去借錢給給巴薩尼歐。

同時，在貝爾蒙，波西亞和她的侍女奈莉莎正在談論波西亞父親設下的抽籤制度，任何想娶波西亞的男士，必須從金、銀或鉛所製的三個箱子做出選擇，選到正確箱子的男士可以贏得波西亞。至今，波西亞都沒有看上任何一個前來追求她的男士。

回到威尼斯，夏洛克答應把巴薩尼歐所需的錢借給安東尼歐，而安東尼歐必須簽下一只借據，上面寫著若安東尼歐無法及時還錢，他得付出自己的一磅肉作為償還。安東尼歐並不因此而擔憂，因為載著他商品的船隻會在借款期限前一個月抵達。

Scene ❶ 🎧

A wharf in Venice, Italy, in the sixteenth century.
Antonio is talking to his friends **Salerio** and **Solanio**.

ANTONIO (*sighing*): I don't know why

    I'm so sad. This mood wearies me.

    You say it wearies you, too.

    But just how I caught it, found it,

      or came by it,

    I do not know. I feel so sad,

    I hardly even know myself.

SALERIO: Your mind is tossing on the ocean.

    (*pointing toward the sea*) It's out there,

    Where your ships with their billowing sails

    Lord it over the common working boats.

SOLANIO: Believe me, if I had taken the risks

    That you have, I would be worried, too.

    Anything that put my investments at risk

    Would make me sad.

SALERIO: As I blew on my hot soup to cool it,

    I'd catch a chill when I thought

    What harm a strong wind might do at sea.

    As I looked at the sand in an hourglass,

I'd think of shallow waters and sandbanks
And see one of my ships stuck in the sand.
Every time I went to church, the holy stones
Would make me think of dangerous rocks.
They'd only have to touch my delicate ship
To scatter all her spices into the sea
And clothe the wild waters with my silks!
One moment I'd be rich—
And the next I'd be worth nothing.
How miserable I would be
If such a thing happened!
You can't fool me. I know Antonio must
Be worrying about his merchandise.

ANTONIO: Believe me, that's not it. I'm lucky.
My investments are not all in one ship
Or all in one place. Nor is all my money
At risk at this time. So my merchandise
Is not what is making me sad.

SOLANIO *(teasing)*: Why, then, you must
Be in love!

ANTONIO *(protesting)*: Not at all!

SOLANIO: Not in love, either? Then let us say
You are sad because you are not merry.
And, if you wanted to, you could laugh.

(**Bassanio**, **Lorenzo**, and **Gratiano** enter.)

Here comes Bassanio, your noble kinsman.

Gratiano and Lorenzo are with him.

(seeing his chance to leave) Farewell!

We'll leave you now with better company.

SALERIO *(also seeing his chance)*:

I would have stayed to cheer you up

If worthier friends had not stopped me.

ANTONIO: That's good of you, but I take it

Your own business calls you.

This gives you the chance to leave.

SALERIO *(to the newcomers)*: Good morning!

BASSANIO *(warmly)*: Gentlemen both!

When shall we have a laugh together, eh?

You're almost strangers! Must it be so?

SALERIO *(eager to get away)*: Yes, yes. We'll get

together one of these days.

(**Salerio** and **Solanio** exit.)

LORENZO: Bassanio, now that you have

Found Antonio, we will leave you.

Remember that we're meeting for dinner.

BASSANIO: I'll be there!

GRATIANO: You don't look well, Antonio.

You let things get you down.

Don't worry so much. Believe me,

You don't seem like yourself lately.

ANTONIO: I take the world as it is, Gratiano,

A stage, where every man must play a part,

And mine a sad one.

GRATIANO: Let me play the fool, then.

Let mirth and laughter give me wrinkles,

And let my emotions get heated with wine

Rather than let my heart cool with sighs.

Why should a warmblooded man

Act like a stone-cold statue of his grandfather?

I tell you what, Antonio—

And I speak out of friendship—

Some men have faces that never change.

They stay still, hoping to be thought of as

Wise, serious, and important. Antonio, I know
    men whose reputation

For being wise is based on saying nothing.

I am very sure that, if they would speak,

They would prove themselves fools.

I'll tell you more about this another time.

But don't go fishing for this fake reputation
With melancholy as your bait, Lorenzo.
(to Antonio): Farewell for now.
I'll end my speech after dinner.

LORENZO: Yes, we'll see you at dinnertime.
I must be one of those silent wise men,
For Gratiano never lets me speak.

GRATIANO: Be my friend two more years—
You'll forget the sound of your own voice!

ANTONIO *(to Gratiano)*: I guess I'd better start
    talking, then.

GRATIANO: If you like. Silence is only good
In dried ox tongues and young maids!

(**Gratiano** and **Lorenzo** exit.)

ANTONIO: What do you think of that?

BASSANIO *(laughing)*: He talks more trash
Than any man in Venice! Any truth
Gratiano speaks is like two grains of wheat
Hidden in two bushels.
Look all day, and when you find them,
They are not worth the search!

ANTONIO: Well, tell me now,

What lady takes your fancy?

You promised to tell me about her today.

BASSANIO *(serious now)*: Antonio, you know

Only too well that I've been spending

My inheritance by living beyond my means.

I'm not angry about having to cut back—

But my main goal is to pay the great debts

that my extravagant living has cost me.

I owe the most to you, Antonio, in money

And in friendship. Because we are friends,

I dare to speak freely about my plans to

Get clear of all the debts I owe.

ANTONIO: Bassanio, tell me everything.

If your plan is honorable—as you are—

Be assured that my purse, my person, and

All my resources are open to you.

BASSANIO: In my schooldays,

If I lost one arrow,

I shot another in the same way. I watched

Its flight carefully to see where the first fell.

By risking both, I often found both.

I tell this childhood story

12

Because my new plan is very similar.
I owe you much and—blame my youth—
What I owe is lost.
But if you would shoot another arrow
The same way you shot the first,
I'll either find both or bring the second one
Back to you again. Then I'll gratefully
Stand by the first debt I owed you.

ANTONIO: You know me well enough.
By doubting that I'd help you, you hurt me
More than if you had wasted all I have.
Just tell me what to do, and I'll do it!

BASSANIO: There is a rich heiress
In Belmont. She is beautiful and virtuous.
Sometimes I have received silent messages
From her eyes. Her name is Portia.
The world is not ignorant of her worth,
For the four winds blow in famous suitors
From every coast. Antonio, if only I had
The money to compete with these suitors,
I'm convinced I could win her hand.

ANTONIO: You know that my wealth is tied up
In cargoes at sea. I do not have the cash,

Nor do I have anything to sell right now.
So go to Venice. See what my credit can do.
Stretch it to the limit to finance your trip
To Belmont and the fair Portia. Go right now
And ask around, and so will I. See
  where money is to be had.
Borrow it on my credit or good name.
Either way, it comes out the same.

(**Bassanio** and **Antonio** exit.)

Scene ❷ 🎧

The hall at Portia's house at Belmont. **Portia** is talking with her maid, **Nerissa**.

PORTIA: Honestly, Nerissa, my little body is weary of this great world.

NERISSA: You would be better off, dear lady, if you had as much misery as you have good fortune. As I see it, those who have too much are as miserable as those who have too little. Excess gives you white hair and makes you old before your time! Moderation leads to a longer life.

PORTIA: Good sentences, and well-said.

NERISSA: They'd be better if well-followed.

PORTIA: If doing were as easy as knowing what to do, poor men's cottages would be palaces. It is a good preacher who follows his own instructions. I'd rather teach twenty how to act than be one of the twenty to follow my own teaching!
The brain might control the emotions, but a hot temper leaps over

a cold rule. Youth ignores good advice because it's a handicap. But all this reasoning won't help me choose a husband. Oh, dear! *(sighing)* That word "choose"! I may neither choose whom I like, nor refuse whom I dislike.
So the will of a living daughter is curbed by the will of a dead father.
Isn't it unfair, Nerissa, that I can neither choose nor refuse?

NERISSA: Your father was very virtuous, and good men are often inspired on their deathbeds. The lottery he set up is a worthy idea. Given a choice of gold, silver, or lead—with you as the prize for the correct choice—only the right man will choose correctly. How do you feel about the princely suitors who have already come to seek your hand?

PORTIA: Please name them. And as you do so, I will describe them for you. Then you can guess by my descriptions how I feel about each of them.

NERISSA: First there is the prince from Naples.

PORTIA: Oh, yes, that colt! He does nothing but talk about his horse. He brags that he can shoe the

beast himself. I suspect
that his mother once had an affair with
a blacksmith!

NERISSA: Then there is the Count Palatine.

PORTIA: He does nothing but frown, as if to say, "If
you won't marry me, choose someone else!" He
listens to jokes and never smiles. I'm sure he'll
be the weeping prophet when he grows old,
being so full of sadness in his youth.
I would rather be married to a skull
than to either of these!

NERISSA: What do you say about the French lord,
Monsieur Le Bon?

PORTIA: Honestly, I know it's a sin to be a mocker—
but him! I would be happy if he hated me, for I
could never return
his love.

NERISSA: And the young English baron?

PORTIA: You know I never speak to him. He doesn't
understand me, and I don't understand him.
He speaks neither Latin, French, nor Italian.
And you know that my English is not good. He

looks manly enough—but who could converse with a dummy? And how oddly he dresses! I think he bought his vest in Italy, his stockings in France, his hat in Germany, and his behavior everywhere!

NERISSA: What about the young German?

PORTIA: I dislike him in the morning when he is sober, and loathe him in the afternoon when he is drunk. When he is at his best, he is less than a man. When he is at his worst, he is little better than a beast.

NERISSA: What if he offers to choose and he chooses the right chest? You would be going against your father's will if you refused to marry him.

PORTIA: Therefore, to prevent the worst, I ask you to set a large glass of Rhine wine on the wrong casket. He'd be tempted to choose that one even if the devil were hidden inside it. I would do anything, Nerissa, before I would marry a sponge!

NERISSA: Dear lady, you need not worry about having any of these lords. They have told me what they have decided. Unless you can be won

by some method other than your father's device of the caskets, they will return to their homes and trouble you no more.

PORTIA: I'll die a virgin unless I'm courted according to my father's will! I'm glad this group of suitors is so reasonable. There's not one of them whose absence
I don't find pleasurable.

NERISSA: Do you remember, dear lady, a suitor from Venice?

PORTIA: Yes, yes! It was Bassanio. At least,
I think that was his name.

NERISSA: True, madam. Of all the men my foolish eyes have ever looked upon, he was the most deserving of a fair lady.

PORTIA: I remember him well. Yes, Bassanio is worthy of your praise.
(A servant enters.) Well, what news?

SERVANT: The four strangers are looking for you, madam, to say goodbye.
A messenger has arrived from a fifth—
the Prince of Morocco. He announces that the prince will be here tonight.

PORTIA: If I can greet the fifth as eagerly
as I can bid the other four farewell,
I'll be glad to see him. Come, Nerissa.
(to the servant): Go on ahead.
(sighing) We no sooner shut the gate on one
wooer than another knocks at it!

(**They** exit.)

Scene ❸ 🎧

A street in Venice, outside Shylock's house. **Bassanio** and **Shylock** are discussing a loan.

SHYLOCK: You want 3,000 ducats . . .

BASSANIO: Yes, sir. For three months.
Antonio will guarantee it. Will you do it?

SHYLOCK *(thinking aloud)*: 3,000 ducats for three
months. Antonio will guarantee it . . .

BASSANIO: What do you say?

SHYLOCK: Antonio is a good man.

BASSANIO: Have you heard differently?

SHYLOCK *(laughing)*: Oh, no, no, no, no!
When I say "a good man," you must
understand that I mean he is good for the
money. But his wealth is at risk.
He has merchant ships going to
Tripoli, the Indies, Mexico, and England—plus
other foreign risks.
But ships are only wood. Sailors are
only men. There are land rats and water rats,
land thieves and water thieves. Pirates, I mean.
And then there are the dangers of waters,

winds, and rocks! Even so, the man is sound.
You say 3,000 ducats? I think I can do it.

BASSANIO: Be assured that you can.

SHYLOCK: I will be assured. What's the latest news
about Antonio's investments? And who is this
coming?

(**Antonio** enters.)

BASSANIO: It's Antonio.

SHYLOCK *(aside):* He looks like a
Fawning innkeeper!
I hate him because he is a Christian.
But I hate him even more because he
Humbly lends out money free of charge,
Bringing down the rate of interest
Here in Venice. If I can catch him unaware,
  I'll pay off old scores very well.
He hates us Jews. He speaks against me,
My deals, and my hard-earned profit,
Which he calls "usury." May my tribe
Be cursed if I ever forgive him!

BASSANIO: Shylock, are you listening?

SHYLOCK: I am figuring out my assets.

By the near guess of my memory,

I cannot instantly raise up the full amount

Of 3,000 ducats. But what of that?

Tubal, a wealthy fellow-Hebrew,

Will help me out. But, wait, I forgot—

When do you plan to pay it back?

(bowing to Antonio) Don't worry, sir,

We were just speaking about you.

ANTONIO: Shylock—although I never

Lend or borrow money with high interest—

I'll make an exception to help my friend.

(to Bassanio): Does he know how much

you want?

SHYLOCK: Yes, yes—3,000 ducats.

ANTONIO: And for three months.

SHYLOCK: I had forgotten. Yes, three months.

You did tell me. Well, then.

Your guarantee . . . let me see . . .

But listen. I thought you said

You never lend or borrow for profit.

ANTONIO: I never do.

SHYLOCK: When Jacob grazed
His Uncle Laban's sheep—

ANTONIO *(impatiently)*: What of him?
Did he take interest?

SHYLOCK: No, he didn't.
Not what you would call direct interest.
Here's what he did. He and Laban agreed
That all the newborn lambs with stripes
And markings would go to Jacob as wages.
When the ewes and the rams were mating,
The skillful shepherd peeled some sticks
And stuck them up in sight of the ewes.
At this point, the ewes conceived.
And so, at lambing time, they dropped
Lambs with stripes and other markings.
Those lambs were Jacob's.
This was a way to profit, and he was blessed.
Profit is a blessing if men don't steal for it.

ANTONIO: Jacob was involved in speculation.
(smiling at Shylock's ignorance) The sticks
Had nothing to do with the outcome.
Did you tell us this to justify profit?

24

Or are you claiming that your
Gold and silver are like ewes and rams?

SHYLOCK: I can't tell, I make it breed as fast!

ANTONIO: Note this, Bassanio. The devil
Can quote Scripture for his own purposes.
An evil man who quotes the Bible
   is like a villain with a smiling face
Or a good apple rotten at the core.
Oh, how attractive falsehood can seem!
Well, Shylock, how about the loan?

SHYLOCK: Antonio, many a time you have
Criticized me for my moneylending.
I've taken it with a patient shrug,
For suffering is the badge of our tribe.
You call me an infidel, a cutthroat dog,
And spit on my Jewish garments.
   All for using what is my own!
Well, now it appears you need my help.
You come to me, and you say, "Shylock,
We'd like some money." You, who spat
On my beard and kicked me as you would
Kick a strange dog out of your house!
   What should I say to you?

"Does a dog have money? Is it possible
That a dog could lend 3,000 ducats?" Or
Should I bow low and say humbly,
"Fair sir, you spat on me last Wednesday.
You spurned me on such-and-such a day.
Another time you called me a dog.
For this, I'll lend you this much money"?

ANTONIO: I am likely to call you so again,
And spit on you and kick you, too!
If you will lend this money, don't lend it
As if to a friend. What kind of friendship
Makes money from a friend?
    Rather, lend it to your enemy.
If he fails to pay you back, you can
More decently impose the penalties.

SHYLOCK: Why, look how you storm!
I want to be friends and have your love,
Forget your shameful treatment,
And supply the money you want, and
    take not a penny of interest.
I'm offering a kindness . . .

BASSANIO: Kindness indeed!

SHYLOCK: This is the kindness I'll show.
Go with me to a lawyer.
Sign an agreement, and—for fun—
If you don't pay me back as agreed,
Let the penalty be a pound of your flesh,
To be cut off and taken from
Whatever part of your body I please.

BASSANIO *(to Antonio)*: You shall not sign
Such a contract for me! I'll manage without.

ANTONIO: Oh, don't worry, man!
In two months—that's one month early—
I expect a return of nine times the value
Of this contract.

SHYLOCK: Oh, Father Abraham!
These Christians! Their own tough bargains
Make them distrust everyone. Tell me this,
If he fails to pay, what would I gain by
The contract? A pound of flesh taken
From a man is not as valuable
As the flesh of sheep, beef, or goats.
I offer this friendship only to buy his good will.
If he takes it, fine. If not, goodbye.
But don't put me in the wrong for this.

ANTONIO: Yes, Shylock. I'll sign the contract.

SHYLOCK: Then meet me at the lawyer's.
Now let me go inside and put the
money together.
I'll join you soon.

(**Shylock** enters his house.)

BASSANIO: I don't trust fair terms
From a villain's mind.

ANTONIO: Come, there's no cause for dismay.
My ships are due a month before the day.

(**They** leave together.)

ACT 2

Summary

在波西亞家中，摩洛哥親王準備要做出選擇。回到威尼斯，年輕的朗西洛特則想離開現任工作，他目前是夏洛克的僕人，但他正在安排轉換去替巴薩尼歐工作。格拉西安諾問巴薩尼歐是否能陪他去貝爾蒙，巴薩尼歐答應了。

當晚，巴薩尼歐準備舉辦一場派對。羅倫佐送了一封信給夏洛克的女兒潔西卡，信中內容是關於他們兩人當晚私奔的事情。夏洛克受邀到巴薩尼歐的派對，他請潔西卡在他出門時把門鎖好。稍晚，羅倫佐與潔西卡在她的陽台下見面，她打扮成男孩的樣子離開父親的家，並偷走一只裝滿父親錢財與珠寶的箱子。

此時在貝爾蒙，摩洛哥親王做出選擇——他選擇金製的箱子——但這選擇是錯的，他必須立刻離開，這讓波西亞大鬆一口氣。在威尼斯，大家都在談論潔西卡與羅倫佐私奔的事。夏洛克在街頭巷尾大吼大叫，要大家幫忙找回他的女兒、錢財和珠寶。同時在貝爾蒙，亞拉岡親王選了銀製的箱子，發現他的選擇也是錯的，因此含淚而去。就在那時，巴薩尼歐出現在波西亞家門前，帶著禮物並準備好要展開追求。

Scene ❶ 🎧

Portia's house in Belmont. The **Prince of Morocco** enters, along with his **attendants**. **Portia**, **Nerissa**, and their **servants** await the visitors.

MOROCCO: Do not dislike me for my color.
　My dark skin is the uniform of those who
　Live under the burning coppery sun.
　Bring me the handsomest man of the north
　Where the sun is barely hot enough
　To thaw the icicles. Then let both of us
　Cut our skin for your love, to prove
　Whose blood is reddest, his or mine.
　I tell you, lady, this face of mine
　Has scared the bravest of men. But I swear
　That the loveliest women of our climate
　Have loved it, too.
　I would not change my color
　Except to win your thoughts, gentle
　　queen.

PORTIA: In terms of choice, I am not led
　By looks alone. Besides, my father's will
　Does not permit me to choose my destiny.
　If my father had not set up these terms,

You, famed prince, would have stood
As good a chance as any I have seen
So far of gaining my love.

MOROCCO: I thank you for that.
Therefore, please lead me to the caskets so
I can try my fortune. To win your love,
I would outstare the sternest eyes,
Pluck the baby cubs from the mother bear,
And even mock the roaring lion. But alas,
   if two champions roll the dice to decide
Who is the greater man, luck may give
The weaker man the higher score. And so,
Blind fortune might cause me to lose what
A lesser man may gain, and die with grief.

PORTIA: You must take your chance.
You must either not make a choice at all,
Or swear before you choose, that if you
Make the wrong choice, never to
Propose marriage to a woman afterwards.
Therefore, think carefully.

MOROCCO: I agree to the conditions.

I'll take my chances.

PORTIA: First you must go to the temple

To swear your oath. After dinner,

You shall have your chance.

MOROCCO: Good luck to me, then!

I'll be either the most blessed or cursed among

men.

(**All** exit.)

————Scene ❷ 🎧————

A street in front of Shylock's house. Shylock's servant **Lancelot Gobbo** enters. He bumps into **Old Gobbo**, his father, who is nearly blind and carrying a basket.

OLD GOBBO: Young master, please help. Which is the way to Master Jew's?

LANCELOT *(aside)*: Oh, heavens! This is my own true father! Being almost blind, he doesn't recognize me. I'll tease him a bit.

(to Old Gobbo): Turn right at the next turning, but left at the next turning of all. At the very next turning, don't turn at all, but turn down indirectly to the Jew's house!

OLD GOBBO: By all the saints, that will be hard to do. Can you tell me if Lancelot is still living with him or not?

LANCELOT *(deciding to reveal himself)*: Don't you recognize me, Father?

OLD GOBBO: Alas, I'm almost blind. I do not.

LANCELOT: Even if you had your sight, you might not know me. It is a wise father that knows his own child. Well, old man, I will tell you news of your son.

I am Lancelot, your boy that was,
Your son that is, your child that shall be.

OLD GOBBO: I can't believe you are my son!

LANCELOT: I don't know how to answer that. But I am Lancelot, and I am sure Margery, your wife, is my mother.

OLD GOBBO: Her name is Margery, indeed. So if you are Lancelot, I'll swear you are my own flesh and blood. Lord, how you've changed! How do you and your master get along? I have brought him a present.

LANCELOT: I've made up my mind to run away. Give him a present? Give him a *noose*! He starves me. My ribs feel like fingers. *(He guides Old Gobbo's hand to his ribs.)* Father, I am glad you've come. Give the present to a certain Master Bassanio. He really does provide smart uniforms! Either I'll serve him or keep running. Look! Here he comes. Go to him, Father. If I serve the Jew any longer, despise me!

(**Bassanio** enters with **Leonardo** and **others**.)

BASSANIO *(to a servant)*: Yes, but be quick about it. I
    want supper ready by five. Deliver these letters.
    Order new uniforms for the servants. Then ask
    Gratiano to come to my house.

(**Servant** exits.)

LANCELOT: Go to him, Father!

OLD GOBBO *(bowing)*: Your worship!

BASSANIO: May I help you?

OLD GOBBO: Here's my son, a poor boy—

LANCELOT *(coming forward)*: Not a poor
    boy, sir, but the rich Jew's servant
    who would like, as my father will
    tell you—

(He hides behind his father.)

OLD GOBBO: He wishes, sir, to serve—

LANCELOT *(coming forward again)*: Well, the
    short and the long of it is that I serve
    the Jew, but I wish to serve you instead.

BASSANIO: I know you well. The job is yours.
    Say goodbye to your old master,
    And go find my house.

LANCELOT: Thank you, sir! Come on, Father.

I'll soon say farewell to the Jew.

(**Lancelot** and his **father** exit. **Gratiano** enters, coming up to **Bassanio**.)

GRATIANO: Bassanio!

BASSANIO: Gratiano!

GRATIANO: I've a favor to ask.

BASSANIO: Granted.

GRATIANO: I must go with you to Belmont.

BASSANIO: Well then, do so. But listen—

Sometimes you are too wild, too rude,

and too bold.

These features suit you well enough

And do not seem like faults to us.

But among strangers, they seem too much.

Please try to tone down your behavior.

Your high spirits might make me

Misunderstood in Belmont

And lose me my hopes.

GRATIANO: Bassanio, listen to me.

If I do not dress soberly, talk with respect,

And swear only now and then, like a man

aiming to please his grandmother—
Never trust me again!

BASSANIO: Very well, we'll see how you act.

GRATIANO: But do not count tonight!
Don't judge me by what we do tonight.

BASSANIO: No, that would be a pity.
I'd rather you were at your funniest,
For our friends want to have a merry time.
But goodbye for now. I have things to do.

GRATIANO: And I must join Lorenzo now.
We will see you at dinner!

(**They** go their separate ways.)

Scene ❸ 🎧

Shylock's front door. **Jessica** and **Lancelot** come out.

JESSICA: I'm sorry you are leaving my father.
But goodbye—here's a ducat for you. And,
Lancelot, please secretly give this letter
To your new master's guest, Lorenzo.

LANCELOT: Goodbye. Let my tears speak for me,
Even though such foolish tears aren't manly.
Goodbye, sweet Jessica!

JESSICA: Farewell, good Lancelot!

(**Lancelot** exits, drying his tears.)

Alas, what a sin it is for me to be ashamed
To be my father's child! I am his daughter,
   But I am not like him.
Oh, Lorenzo, if you keep your promise,
There will be an end to this strife,
I'll become a Christian, and your
   loving wife.

(**She** goes indoors.)

Scene 4 🎧

Another street in Venice. **Gratiano**, **Lorenzo**, **Salerio**, and **Solanio** enter, discussing preparations for their fancy-dress party.

LORENZO: So we will leave at suppertime,

Change our clothes at my lodging,

And be back within the hour.

GRATIANO: But we have not prepared well.

SALERIO: We haven't hired torchbearers.

SOLANIO: It's stupid unless organized well.

I don't think we should do it.

LORENZO: It's only 4:00. We have two hours

To get everything ready.

(**Lancelot** enters.)

Friend Lancelot, what's the news?

LANCELOT *(producing a letter)*: Open this, and you'll know.

GRATIANO: A love letter, I see!

LANCELOT: Excuse me, sir.

(He starts to leave.)

LORENZO: Where are you going?

LANCELOT: Well, sir, to invite my old master, the Jew, to dine tonight with my new master, the

Christian.

LORENZO: Hold on. Take this.

(He gives him a tip.) Tell dear Jessica

I will not fail her. Tell her privately.

(**Lancelot** leaves.)

Go, gentlemen. Get ready for tonight.

SALERIO: Right. I'll get started on it.

SOLANIO: So will I.

LORENZO: Meet me and Gratiano

At Gratiano's place in about an hour.

SALERIO: Good idea.

(**Salerio** and **Solanio** leave.)

GRATIANO: Was that letter from fair Jessica?

LORENZO: I'd better tell you all. She told me

The way to take her from her father's house,

What gold and jewels she will bring,

And how she will dress as a page.

If ever her father enters heaven,

It will be because of his gentle daughter.

May misfortune never cross her path.

Come with me. Read this as you go along.

Fair Jessica will be my torchbearer!

(**They** walk off briskly.)

Scene 5 🎧

Shylock enters with **Lancelot**.

SHYLOCK: Well, you'll see! Your eyes
   Will judge the difference between
   Old Shylock and Bassanio.
   (calling out): *Jessica!*
   (to Lancelot): You won't stuff yourself as
   You have with me. *(calling again) Jessica!*
   (to Lancelot): Or sleep and snore,
   And wear out your clothes. *(calling louder)*
   What, Jessica, I say!

(**Jessica** enters.)

JESSICA: Did you call? What is your wish?

SHYLOCK: I'm invited out to dinner, Jessica.
   Here are my keys. But why should I go?
   I'm not invited out of love. They flatter me.
   But still, I'll go in hate, to eat the food of
   The wasteful Christian. Jessica, my girl,
   Look after my house. I don't want to go.
   Something doesn't feel quite right.

LANCELOT: I beg you, sir, *go!* My young master
   expects the displeasure of your company.

SHYLOCK: As I do his.

LANCELOT: And they have planned something. I
won't say exactly that you'll see a masque. But
(winking) if you *do* see one
of those dramas, don't be surprised.

SHYLOCK: What, will there be a masque?
Listen, Jessica. Lock my doors. When
You hear the drum and the vile squealing
Of the fife player, don't look out
Into the street to see Christian fools
In painted masks. Plug my house's ears—
Don't let the sound of shallow foolishness
Enter my sober home.
I swear I have no wish to dine out tonight,
But I will go.
(to Lancelot): Go ahead, you. Say I'll come.

LANCELOT: I'll go ahead, sir.
(aside to Jessica): Miss, look out the window
because *(reciting)*
> *A certain Christian will come by,*
> *Worth the sight of a Jewess's eye.*

(**He** leaves, whistling.)

SHYLOCK: What did that fool Gentile say?

JESSICA: He said, "Farewell, miss." No more.

SHYLOCK: The fool is kind enough,
But a huge eater, a snail-slow worker,
And he sleeps more by day than a wildcat.
I'll have no lazy ones in my house,
So I let him go—to someone he can help
    waste borrowed money.
Jessica, go in. I may return immediately.
Do as I say. Shut the doors behind you.

(**Shylock** leaves.)

JESSICA: Farewell. If my luck is not crossed,
I've a father and you've a daughter lost.

(**Jessica** goes inside.)

Scene 6 🎧

A street in Venice. **Gratiano** and **Salerio** enter, wearing masks.

GRATIANO: This is the balcony under which

Lorenzo asked us to wait.

SALERIO: He's late.

GRATIANO: It is strange that he's not here.

Lovers are usually early.

SALERIO: Look! Here he comes now.

(**Lorenzo** enters.)

LORENZO: Good friends, forgive my lateness.

It was business, not myself, that caused it.

Come. This is where my Jewish father

lives.

(He calls out.) Hello! Anybody home?

(A window opens, and **Jessica** appears, dressed as a boy.)

JESSICA: Who's that? Although I think

I know your voice, say who you are!

LORENZO: Lorenzo, and your love!

JESSICA: Lorenzo certainly, and my love

For sure! Here, catch this chest.

It's worth the trouble.

(**She** throws it down.)

45

I'm glad it is night. Don't look at me,
For I am ashamed to show my clothes.
But love is blind, and lovers cannot see
Their own foolishness. If they could,
Cupid himself would blush
To see me changed into a boy.

LORENZO: Come down.

You must be my torchbearer.

JESSICA: Must I hold a candle to my shame?

Indeed, it shines out quite enough

as it is.

Love thrives in modesty,

And I should be concealed.

LORENZO: And so you are, my sweet.

Even in the lovely disguise of a boy.

But come at once. It's getting late,

And we are expected at Bassanio's

party.

(**She** closes the window.)

(to Gratiano): By heaven, I love her dearly!

If I'm any judge, she's wise, and

If my eyes tell the truth, she's beautiful!

That she is faithful, she has just proved.

Therefore her image—wise, beautiful,

and faithful

Resides in my constant soul.

(**Jessica** comes out of the house.)

You are here, then. Come on, gentlemen!

Our friends are waiting for us at the party.

(**They** set off for the party.)

Scene 7

The hall of Portia's house in Belmont. **Portia** enters, with the **Prince of Morocco** and their **servants** and **attendants**.

PORTIA *(to servant)*: Go, open the curtains.

Show the noble prince the three caskets.

(The curtains are drawn back, revealing three caskets displayed on a table.)

(to the prince): Now make your choice.

MOROCCO: The first, gold, bears the words:

"*Who chooses me*

Shall gain what many men desire."

The second, silver, carries this promise:

"*Who chooses me*

Shall get as much as he deserves."

The third, of dull lead, bluntly warns:

"*Who chooses me*

Must give and gamble all he has."

How shall I know if my choice is right?

PORTIA: One of these contains my picture,

Prince. If you choose that, you will be

my husband.

MOROCCO: May some god guide me!

Let me see. What does this lead casket say?

"*. . . must give and gamble all he has.*"

Must give? For what? For lead?
Risk all for lead? This casket looks
Dangerous. I'll not give or risk all for lead.
What about the silver one?

"*. . . shall get as much as he deserves.*"

Pause there, Morocco. Weigh your value.
I deserve enough, but "enough"
Might not stretch as far as to the lady.
And yet I should not underestimate myself.
As much as I deserve—Why, that's the lady!
What if I went no further, but chose here?
Let's see once more the saying on the gold.

"*. . . shall gain what many men desire.*"

That's the lady—all the world desires her.
One of the three holds her heavenly picture.
Is it likely that lead contains her?
I don't think so. Nor do I think she's in
The silver, which is worth less than gold.
Give me the key. I choose the gold one,
And take my chance!

PORTIA *(handing him the key)*: Take it, Prince.

If my picture is inside, then I am yours.

(**He** opens the golden casket.)

MOROCCO: Oh, no! What have we here?

A rotting skull, with a rolled-up manuscript
stuffed

In its empty eye socket. I'll read it.

"All that glitters is not gold;
Often you have heard that told.
Many a man his life has sold,
Just my outside to behold.
Golden tombs do worms enfold.
Had you been as wise as bold,
Young in limbs, in wisdom old,
Your answer would not be enscrolled—
Fare you well. Your suit is cold.
Cold indeed, and labor lost.
So farewell heat, and welcome frost."

Portia, goodbye! I have too sad a heart

For a long farewell. Thus losers depart.

(Bowing, **he** leaves with his **attendants**.)

PORTIA *(to Nerissa)*: Good riddance!

(to servant): Close the curtains. Go.

May all with his vanity leave me so.

(**They** exit.)

Scene 8 🎧 13

A street in Venice. **Salerio** and **Solanio** enter.

SALERIO: Why, man, I saw Bassanio set sail.
Gratiano has gone along with him.
I am sure Lorenzo is not on board.

SOLANIO: The villainous Jew with his outcries
Roused the duke, who went with him
To search Bassanio's ship.

SALERIO: He was too late. The ship was gone.
But someone said that Lorenzo and Jessica
Were seen together in a gondola.
Besides, Antonio told the duke that
They were not with Bassanio in his ship.

SOLANIO: I never heard such an outcry
As the Jew did utter in the streets.
"My daughter! My ducats! My daughter!
Fled with a Christian! Justice! The law!
My ducats, and my daughter! A sealed bag!
Two bags of golden ducats
Stolen from me by my daughter!
And jewels—two precious stones—

Stolen by my daughter! Find the girl!
She has the stones and the money!"

SALERIO *(laughing)*: All the boys in Venice
Follow him, crying, "His stones!
His daughter! His money!"

SOLANIO *(serious now)*: Antonio had better
Pay his loan on time, or he will pay for this.

SALERIO: You're right.
I chatted with a Frenchman yesterday,
Who said that a rich Venetian ship had
Foundered in the English Channel.
I thought about Antonio when he told me,
And wished in silence that it wasn't his.

SOLANIO: You'd better tell Antonio about it.
But do it gently. It may grieve him.

SALERIO: There's no kinder man on earth!
I saw Bassanio and Antonio part.
Bassanio said he'd return quickly.
Antonio said, "Do not hurry for my sake.
Stay as long as you must. As for the
Jew's contract, don't let it affect
Your love plans. Be merry, and focus

ACT 2
SCENE
8

On courtship and such shows of love
That seem proper there." At this point,
His eyes filled with tears. Turning his face,
He put his hand out behind him, and with
Great affection, he shook Bassanio's hand.
And so they parted.

SOLANIO: I think he means the world to him.
Let's go find him and cheer him up.

SALERIO: Let's do that.

(**They** leave.)

Scene ❾

Portia's house at Belmont. The casket room. **Nerissa** and a **servant** enter.

NERISSA: Quick! Please draw the curtain!

The Prince of Aragon has taken his oath,

And he's coming to make his choice now.

(The **servant** closes the curtains. **Portia**, the **Prince of Aragon**, and their **attendants** enter.)

PORTIA: There are the caskets, noble Prince.

If you choose the one with my picture in it,

We shall be married right away.

But if you fail, you must leave immediately.

ARAGON: I know the risk. May fortune now

Grant me my heart's hope!

Gold, silver, and base lead.

"Who chooses me

Must give and gamble all he has."

(addressing the lead casket): You must

Look fairer before I'd give and gamble all.

What does the golden chest say?

"Who chooses me

Shall gain what many men desire."

I will not choose what many men desire,
Because I am not like the common masses.
Well then, to you, silver treasure house!
Tell me once more what you say.
   "Who chooses me
      Shall get as much as he deserves."
That is my choice. Give me the key for this.
(**He** opens the silver casket.)

What's here? The portrait of a fool,
Offering me a note. I will read it.
(looking at the picture) How unlike you
Are to Portia! How unlike my hopes and
My deservings! Did I deserve no more
Than a clown's head?
(opening the document and reading)

   "Some there are that shadows kiss,
      Some have but a shadow's bliss.
   There are fools alive, I say,
   Who are silvered over in this way.
   It matters not which wife you wed,
   I will always be your head.
   So be off, for you are sped."
   (to Portia): A greater fool I shall appear

The longer that I linger here.

With one fool's head I came to woo,

But I go away with two.

Sweet, farewell, my word I'll keep,

To bear with patience my sorrows deep.

(**He** leaves with his **attendants**.)

PORTIA *(relieved)*: Another moth burned

By the candle! Oh, these pompous fools!

Thinking they can so wisely choose,

They're so surprised when they lose.

NERISSA: The old words said it straight—

To hang or to marry is a matter of fate.

PORTIA: Come, draw the curtain, Nerissa.

(She does so. A **servant** enters.)

SERVANT: Madam, a young Venetian is here.

He has brought gifts of great value.

Until now I have not seen so promising

An ambassador of love.

PORTIA: Come, Nerissa, for I long to see this

Messenger of Cupid who seems so gentle.

NERISSA: May it be Bassanio, Lord willing!

(**All** exit.)

ACT 3

Summary

威尼斯傳來安東尼歐有許多船隻沉沒的消息,夏洛克決心要逼安東尼歐履行合約,以報復所有安東尼歐以前對自己的羞辱。在貝爾蒙,巴薩尼歐做出選擇——鉛製寶箱——並發現他的選擇是正確的。波西亞非常開心,因為巴薩尼歐是她唯一喜歡的追求者。格拉西安諾也坦承,若巴薩尼歐選對箱子,奈莉莎將願意嫁給他。

一封來自安東尼歐的信,上面宣告著他的苦境,因為夏洛克想要得到他的一磅肉。波西亞和巴薩尼歐立刻成婚,格拉西安諾和奈莉莎也追隨兩人腳步。同一天,巴薩尼歐前往威尼斯以幫助安東尼歐。在威尼斯,安東尼歐試圖與夏洛克講道理,但夏洛克依然堅持要履行合約。

此時,波西亞要羅倫佐在她與奈莉莎離家時幫忙顧家,她說她和奈莉莎要去修道院禱告,直到她們的丈夫回來——但實際上,波西亞有別的打算。

Scene ❶ 🎧

The street in front of Shylock's house in Venice. **Solanio** meets **Salerio**, who has just come from the Rialto, the business center.

SOLANIO: What's the news on the Rialto?

SALERIO: There's a story going around
That one of Antonio's ships has been
Wrecked in the English Channel.

SOLANIO: What's that? He's lost a ship?

SALERIO: I hope it's the end of his losses.

SOLANIO: Let me say "Amen" at once,
In case the devil thwarts my prayer,
For here he comes in the form of a Jew.

(**Shylock** comes out of his house.)

Well now, Shylock! What's the news?

SHYLOCK *(angrily)*: You knew—none so well
as you—of my daughter's flight.

SALERIO: Of course! I even knew the tailor
Who made the wings for her!

SOLANIO: Shylock knew the bird was ready
To fly—and that it is natural
For young birds to leave their mothers.

SHYLOCK: She is damned for it!

SALERIO: Oh, yes, if the devil is her judge.

SHYLOCK: My own flesh and blood to rebel!

SOLANIO *(pretending to misunderstand)*: Fancy that,
old skin and bones.
What, at your age?

SHYLOCK: I mean my daughter, who is my flesh and
blood.

SALERIO: Your flesh and hers are
More different than jet black and ivory.
Your bloods are more different
Than red wine and white.
But tell us now—have you heard whether
Antonio has had any loss at sea?

SHYLOCK: There I made another bad deal.
A bankrupt. A prodigal. He hardly dares to
Show his face on the Rialto. A beggar now,
Who used to come so smugly to town.
He'd better honor his bond!

SALERIO: Well, I'm sure if he can't,
You won't take his flesh.
After all, what is it good for?

60

SHYLOCK: To bait fish with! If it will feed

Nothing else, it will feed my revenge.

He has disgraced me, hindered me,

Laughed at my losses, mocked my gains.

He has scorned my nationality,

Thwarted my deals, cooled my friends,

Angered my enemies. And why?

I am a Jew. But hasn't a Jew got eyes?

Doesn't a Jew have hands, organs, limbs,

Senses, affections, passions?

Isn't he fed with the same food,

Hurt by the same weapons,

Subject to the same diseases,

Healed by the same means,

Warmed and cooled by the

Same winter and summer, as a Christian is?

If you prick us, do we not bleed?

If you tickle us, do we not laugh?

If you poison us, do we not die?

And if you wrong us,

Shall we not seek revenge?

If we are like you in everything else,

We will be like you in that.

If a Jew wrongs a Christian,
What is his natural response? Revenge.
If a Christian wrongs a Jew, what should
His penalty be—by Christian example?
Why, revenge!
The villainy you teach me, I will carry out.
And I'll go one better if I get the chance!

(A **servant** stops **Solanio** and **Salerio**.)

SERVANT: Sirs, my master Antonio is at home.
He would like to speak to you both.

SALERIO: We've been looking for him.

(**Solanio**, **Salerio**, and the **servant** leave. **Tubal** comes toward Shylock's house.)

SHYLOCK: Greetings, Tubal. What news
From Genoa? Did you find my daughter?

TUBAL: I heard her spoken of,
But I could not find her.

SHYLOCK: No news of them? All right.
And I don't know what the search
Has cost so far. Loss upon loss!
The thief gone with so much, and
So much more spent to find the thief,
yet no satisfaction! No revenge!

No bad luck anywhere

Except what falls on my shoulders.

No sighs but my sighs. No tears but mine!

(**He** cries.)

TUBAL: Yes, other men have bad luck, too.

Antonio, as I heard in Genoa . . .

SHYLOCK *(recovering quickly)*: What, what?

Bad luck? Bad luck, you say?

TUBAL: He's lost a ship coming from Tripoli.

SHYLOCK: I thank God! Is it true?

TUBAL: I spoke to some of the sailors

Who escaped from the wreck.

SHYLOCK: Thank you, Tubal. Good news!

Ha, ha! You heard this in Genoa?

TUBAL *(changing the subject)*: I also heard

That your daughter spent eighty ducats

in one night.

SHYLOCK: You stick a dagger in me!

I shall never see my gold again.

Eighty ducats at a sitting! Eighty ducats!

TUBAL *(switching back again)*: Several of
Antonio's creditors came to me in Venice.
They swear he'll soon be bankrupt.

SHYLOCK: I'm glad of it. I'll plague him.
I'll torture him. I'm glad of it!

TUBAL *(getting back to Jessica)*: One of them
Showed me a ring that your daughter
Had traded with him for a monkey.

SHYLOCK: You torture me, Tubal!
Leah gave me that ring before we married.
I would not have traded it
For a wilderness of monkeys.

TUBAL *(trying to ease Shylock's pain)*: But Antonio is
certainly ruined.

SHYLOCK: Yes, that's true. Go, find a sheriff.
I'll give Antonio two weeks' notice.
If he can't pay, I'll have his heart!
Once he's out of Venice, I can do business
My own way. Go, Tubal—and meet me
At our synagogue.

(**They** leave, going separate ways.)

Scene ❷ 🎧

The hall of Portia's house at Belmont. The curtains are drawn back, revealing the caskets. **Bassanio** is ready to make his choice.

PORTIA: Wait a little, please. Pause a day

Or two before you take the gamble. If you

Choose wrong, I'll lose your company.

Therefore, wait a while. Something tells me

   that I don't want to lose you.

You know yourself that hatred does not

Give such advice. But in case you do not

Understand me well—for maidens can only

Think their thoughts, not speak them—

I'd like to keep you here a month or two

   before you make your choice.

I could teach you how to choose right,

But I'm under oath not to. If you don't win,

I'll never be another's. If you should fail,

You'll make me wish something sinful—

That I had broken my oath and advised you.

   Shame on your eyes!

They've looked at me, dividing me in two.

Half of me is yours. The other half, too.

I ought to say "my own," but what is mine
Is yours, so all of me is yours.
I talk too much, but it's to slow down time,
Draw it out, and stretch out its length
To delay the making of your choice.

BASSANIO: Let me choose.
As I am, I'm living on the rack of torment.

PORTIA: On the rack, Bassanio! Confess then
What treason is mingled with your love!

BASSANIO: Only the ugly treason of mistrust,
Which makes me fear enjoying my love.
Snow and fire might just as well be friends,
As treason and my love.

PORTIA: Yes, but I'm afraid the rack makes
You say anything, like any tortured man.

BASSANIO: Promise me life,
And I'll confess the truth!

PORTIA: Well then, confess and live.

BASSANIO: "Confess and love" would be my
Full confession. Oh, happy torment,
When my torturer gives me the answers
To set me free. But let me
Test my fortune with the caskets.

PORTIA: Go then! I am locked in one of them.

If you really love me, you will find me.

(to the onlookers): Nerissa and the rest,

Stand aside. Let music play as he chooses.

That way, if he loses, he can leave

Like a dying swan, fading in music.

(One **servant** stays while the others go to the musicians' gallery.)

To extend the comparison, my tears will be

The stream and watery deathbed for him.

(more cheerfully) He may win.

What of music then? Oh, then, music would be

   like the dawn chorus that

Creeps into the dreaming bridegroom's ear,

Calling him to his wedding. There he goes,

(to Bassanio): Go, love! If you win, I live!

(Music plays while **Bassanio** thinks.)

BASSANIO: The world is fooled by ornament.

In law, any plea, no matter how corrupt,

Can hide its evil behind a saintly voice.

In religion, any heresy can be blessed by

Some learned man who uses the Scriptures

   in support of its grossness.

How many cowards, with hearts as false
As stairs made from sand, sport beards
Like brave Hercules and warlike Mars?
They only wear those beards to seem tough.
   Look on beauty. You'll see that it's often
Purchased by the ounce.
Cosmetics work miracles. Those with the
Lightest morals use them most heavily.
Ornament is the rocky shore of a most
Dangerous sea, the beautiful scarf veiling
An uncertain beauty. Therefore, gaudy gold,
   I want none of you. Nor of you, silver,
The stuff of common coins. But you,
Worthless lead, which threatens
Rather than promises, your paleness
Moves me more than eloquence.
   I choose you. May joy be the result!

(The **servant** hands him the key.)

PORTIA *(aside):* How fast all other passions
   Disappear—doubt, despair, fear,
   And green-eyed jealousy! Oh, love,
   Be moderate, control your ecstasy,
   Restrain your joy! Don't get too excited—

68

I feel your blessing too much. Make it less,
In case it overwhelms me!

BASSANIO *(opening the casket)*: What's this?
Fair Portia's portrait! *(admiring it)* Divine!
Do these eyes move? Or do they merely
Reflect the motion of mine? Here are lips
Parted with sugar breath! Here in her hair
  the painter has, like a spider,
Woven a golden net to entrap men's hearts,
Faster than gnats in cobwebs. But her eyes!
How could he see to do them? After he
Painted one, it would have had the power to
Blind him, denying itself a companion.
  But look! Just as my praises undervalue
The portrait, so does this portrait
Fall short of the reality. Here's the scroll,
On which my fortune is summarized:
(**He** reads the scroll.)

> "You who choose not by the view
>   Take fair chance, and choose quite true.
>   Since this fortune falls to you,
>   Be content, seek nothing new.
>   If you be well-pleased with this

And see your fortune as your bliss,
Turn to where your lady is,
And claim her with a loving kiss."
A kindly scroll! *(He turns to Portia.)*
I come to you with a permit, by your
   leave,
(offering the scroll as a permit for a kiss)
A kiss to give and to receive.
But only if this is agreeable to you.
I wait to hear your answer true.

PORTIA: You see me, Lord Bassanio, as I am.
   For myself, I would not seek improvement.
   But for you, I wish I were 60 times better,
   A thousand times more beautiful,
   Ten thousand times richer.
      I'm really very little—at best
   An uneducated and inexperienced girl.
   Happily, not too old to learn.
   Happier still, not too stupid to learn.
   Happiest of all—I surrender myself to you,
   My lord, governor, and king.
(**They** kiss, meeting the terms of the scroll.)
   Myself, and what is mine, are now yours.

70

Until now I was the lord of this fine house,
Master of my servants, queen over myself.
Now, this house, these servants, and myself
Are yours. I give them with this ring.

(**She** puts a ring on Bassanio's finger.)

If you part with it, lose it, or give it away,
That will mean the end of your love
And be my reason to denounce you.

BASSANIO: Madam, I don't know what to say!
Only the blood in my veins speaks to you.
I am like a crowd of people overwhelmed
by the fine speech of a beloved prince.
Every atom of my being is shouting with
Wild cheers of joy. When this ring
Parts from this finger, life parts from me.
Then you could confidently say,
"This means that Bassanio is dead."

(**Nerissa** and **Gratiano** join them.)

NERISSA: Good joy, my lord and lady!

GRATIANO: Lord Bassanio and gentle lady,
I wish you great joy. And when the time
Comes for your wedding, I beg you
That at that time I can be married, too!

BASSANIO: Of course—if you can find a wife.

GRATIANO: Thanking your lordship,
　　You have found me one.

(**He** takes Nerissa's hand.)

　　My eyes, my lord, are just as swift as yours.
　　You saw the mistress—I spotted the maid.
　　You loved, I loved.
　　Your fortune depended on the caskets there,
　　And so did mine, as it happened.
　　I wooed until I sweated, and swore
　　Oaths of love until my mouth ran dry.
　　At last I got a promise of her hand
　　From this fair lady here,
　　On condition that you won her mistress.

PORTIA: Is this true, Nerissa?

NERISSA: Madam, it is, if you are pleased.

BASSANIO: Do you mean it, Gratiano?

GRATIANO: Yes indeed, my lord.

BASSANIO: Our wedding feast will be
　　Most honored by your marriage.

GRATIANO *(to Nerissa)*: We'll bet them
　　A thousand ducats that we have a son first.

NERISSA *(blushing)*: What, betting on that?

GRATIANO *(teasing)*: We'll never win,

If we don't get started soon!

(**Lorenzo** and **Jessica** enter, followed by **Salerio**, who is carrying a letter.)

But who's this? Lorenzo and Jessica?

What—and my old Venetian friend, Salerio?

BASSANIO: Lorenzo and Salerio, welcome.

If one so new in my status here can do so,

I bid you welcome.

(to Portia): With your permission, sweet Portia.

PORTIA: They are entirely welcome, my lord.

LORENZO *(to Bassanio)*: I thank your honor.

For my part, I did not plan to see you here.

But I met Salerio on the way,

And he begged me to come along.

He wouldn't take no for an answer.

SALERIO: I did, my lord, with good reason.

(**He** gives **Bassanio** the letter.)

Antonio sends his respects.

BASSANIO: Before I open his letter,

Tell me how my good friend is doing.

SALERIO: Not sick—unless it's in his mind.

Yet not well either, unless you mean mentally.

His letter explains his situation.

(**Bassanio** opens the letter.)

GRATIANO *(nodding toward Jessica):* Nerissa,

Cheer up our stranger. Bid her welcome.

(**Nerissa** greets **Jessica**, while **Gratiano** shakes hands with **Salerio**.)

Your hand, Salerio. What's new in Venice?

How is Antonio getting along?

I know he will be happy for us!

SALERIO: He'll be happy for you, I'm sure.

But things are not going so well for him.

(He takes Gratiano to one side to explain.)

PORTIA *(observing Bassanio as he reads):* There are

some sad contents in that letter

That rob the color from Bassanio's cheek.

Some dear friend dead? What—worse?

(She touches his arm.) With respect,

Bassanio, I am half yourself. I will freely

Share half of any trouble this letter brings you.

BASSANIO: Sweet Portia! Here are some of the

Saddest words that ever blotted paper!

Dear lady, when I first told you of my love,
I freely confessed that all my wealth
Ran in my veins. I was a gentleman,
So I told you the truth. And yet, dear lady,
When I told you I had nothing, you will see
That I was bragging. I should have told you
That I had less than nothing. Actually,
I am indebted to a dear friend, who lent me
Money borrowed from his worst enemy.

Here is a letter, lady.
The paper represents my friend's body,
And every word in it is a gaping wound,
Leaking his life's blood. But is it true,
Salerio, that all his investments have failed?
Not one success? From Tripoli, Mexico,
England? From Lisbon, Barbary, India?
Not one ship escaped the dreadful touch of
Shipwrecking rocks?

SALERIO: Not one, my lord. Besides, it seems
That even if he could pay the loan,
The Jew would not take the money.
I never knew a creature in human form
   so sharp and hungry to destroy a man.
He appeals to the duke morning and night.

He says it is unlawful to deny him justice.
The duke, the nobles, and 20 merchants
Have argued with him. But he won't listen.

JESSICA: When I lived with him, I heard him
Swear that he'd rather have Antonio's flesh
Than 20 times the amount he owes.
I know, my lord, that if law, authority,
And power don't stop him,
It will go hard with poor Antonio.

PORTIA: Is Antonio your dear friend?

BASSANIO: My dearest friend.
The kindest man, the best meaning
And most tireless of those
Who do good deeds. He is one with more
Roman honor in him than any man in Italy.

PORTIA: How much does he owe the Jew?

BASSANIO: On my behalf, 3,000 ducats.

PORTIA: No more? Pay him 6,000! No,
Two times that. And then three times that!
No friend of that description
Shall lose a hair through Bassanio's fault.
First go with me to church and call me wife.
Then go to Venice to your friend.

<blockquote>
You shall not lie by Portia's side

With a troubled spirit. Take enough gold

To pay the petty debt 20 times over.

When it is paid, bring your true friend here.

Nerissa and I will live as maids and widows

Until you come back. Away, now!

You must leave on your wedding day.

Bid welcome to your friends. Smile!

Since you are dearly bought,

I'll love you dearly.

Let me hear your friend's letter.
</blockquote>

BASSANIO *(reading)*: *"Dear Bassanio, my ships have all been wrecked. My creditors grow cruel. My assets are very low. My bond to the Jew is forfeit. In paying it, I cannot possibly live. But all debts between us will be cleared—if, at my death, I could but see you. Even so, do as you wish. If your love for me does not persuade you to come, don't let this letter do so."*

PORTIA: Oh, my love! Hurry to him!

BASSANIO: Since you have given your consent,

I'll go. But, until I return, I will

Neither sleep nor rest!

*(**Everyone** hurries off.)*

Scene ③ 🎧

Outside Shylock's house. **Shylock** stands at his door, with **Antonio**, **Solanio**, and **Jailer**.

SHYLOCK: Jailer, guard him well!
Don't talk to me of mercy!
This is the fool who lent out money
Free of interest. Jailer, guard him.

ANTONIO: Listen a minute, good Shylock—

SHYLOCK: I will have my bond! Don't speak
Against my bond. I've sworn an oath
That I will have my bond. You called me
a dog before you had a reason.
Since I am a dog, beware my fangs!
The duke will grant me justice. I'm amazed,
You wicked jailer, that you are so foolish
As to wander about with him at his request!

ANTONIO: Please, hear me speak!

SHYLOCK: *I'll have my bond.* Do not speak!
I'll not be made into a soft and stupid fool,
Shaking my head, sighing, and giving in
To Christian pleas. Don't follow me.
Don't speak to me! I will have my bond!

78

(**He** enters his house, slamming the door.)

SOLANIO: He's the most stubborn dog

Who ever kept company with men.

ANTONIO: Leave him alone.

I'll follow him no more with useless pleas.

He wants my life. I know his reason well.

I often paid others' debts to him when

They asked me for help. So he hates me.

SOLANIO: I'm sure the duke will never
Rule in favor of the terms of this bond.

ANTONIO: The duke cannot change the law.
If we denied the rights of strangers
Here in Venice, it would go against
Our ideas of justice. The city trades
With people of all nations.
I've lost so much weight
Because of my griefs and losses
That tomorrow I can hardly spare a pound
Of flesh to my bloodthirsty creditor.
Well, jailer, let's move on. If only
Bassanio will come to see me pay his debt.
Then I shall be content!

(**They** exit.)

Scene ❹ 🎧18

Portia's house in Belmont. **Portia**, **Nerissa**, **Lorenzo**,
Jessica, and Portia's servant **Balthazar** enter.

LORENZO: Madam, you have a truly noble
　Understanding of friendship.
　If you knew the man you are honoring—
　How true a gentleman he is, how dearly
　He loves your husband—I know you
　Would be even prouder of what you did.

PORTIA: I've never regretted doing good
　And do not now. Between friends
　Who talk and spend time together,
　And who love each other equally,
　There must be a similarity in spirit.
　This makes me think that Antonio,
　　being a close friend of my husband,
　Must be like him. If that is so,
　How cheaply have I rescued a soulmate
　From hellish cruelty. This sounds too much
　Like praising myself, so that's enough!
　　To change the subject, Lorenzo,
　I want you to take over the management
　Of my household until my husband returns.
　For myself, I've made a secret vow to live

Alone in prayer and contemplation,
Except for Nerissa here,
Until our husbands return.
There is a monastery two miles away. We'll live there.
I hope you won't deny my request,
Which I ask out of love and pressing need.

LORENZO: Madam, with my whole heart,
I shall obey all of your commands.

PORTIA: My servants already know my plans.
They will accept you and Jessica
In place of Lord Bassanio and myself.
So farewell until we meet again!

LORENZO: Farewell to you, dear lady.

(**Jessica** and **Lorenzo** exit.)

PORTIA: Now, Balthazar! You've always been
Honest and true. Let me find you so now.
(handing him a letter) Take this letter,
And get to Padua as fast as you can.
Give this to my cousin, Doctor Bellario,
And he'll give you certain documents
And clothing. Bring them to the crossing
Where the public ferry trades with Venice.
Waste no time in words, but just go!
I'll be there before you.

BALTHAZAR: Madam, I'll go quickly.

(**He** leaves.)

PORTIA: Come on, Nerissa. I have work to do
That you do not know about. We'll see
Our husbands before they think of us.

NERISSA: Will they see us?

PORTIA: They will, Nerissa, but they'll think,
By our clothes, that we are male. I will bet you that
When we're dressed as young men,
I will be the handsomer of the two.
I'll wear my dagger more bravely, speak in
The high-pitched voice of an adolescent,
Turn my maidenly steps into a manly stride,
And boast of brawls like a bragging youth.
I'll lie about how many hearts I've broken,
So that people will swear that I left school
At least twelve months ago.

NERISSA: What—are we to turn into men?

PORTIA: Dear me! What a silly question!
But come. I'll tell you my plan when we're
In my coach, which waits at the park gate.
Let's hurry. We must cover twenty miles today!

(**They** rush away.)

ACT 4

Summary

在威尼斯,夏洛克堅持履行合約是法律賦予他的權利。公爵建議夏洛克展現慈悲之心,但夏洛克斷然拒絕。波西亞和奈莉莎穿著法學博士和法官書記員的服裝,手裡拿著偽造的介紹信。公爵同意讓波西亞解決這個案子。

波西亞力勸夏洛克憐憫安東尼歐,並給他許多機會,希望他能收下三倍欠款的錢,將此債務一筆勾銷,但夏洛克卻屢屢拒絕。波西亞終於同意夏洛克可以去取一磅的肉——但條件是他不能讓安東尼歐流下一滴血,或是多取下一盎司的二十分之一的肉。夏洛克終於說他接受三倍的錢,但波西亞卻說他已錯過接受的機會。現在夏洛克只能選擇冒險履行借據,或是放棄一切。除此之外,法律規定,若一個人意圖謀取任何威尼斯市民的性命,必須受到處罰,他將失去所有財產,一半要給被他意圖傷害的人,另一半收歸公庫。而且,他的命也掌握在公爵手裡。公爵饒夏洛克一命,並將他的一半財產歸給安東尼歐。國家判定夏洛克可以留住他一半的財產,但他必須在死後將這筆錢留給他的女兒和女婿,他也必須立刻成為基督徒。夏洛克同意了這些條件。

假法官波西亞要巴薩尼歐給她戒指當作此事的報酬,波西亞曾要求巴薩尼歐絕不能跟戒指分離。在安東尼歐的勸說之下,巴薩尼歐把戒指給了她。

Scene ❶ 🎧

A court of law in Venice. **Antonio** enters between two **guards**, followed by **Bassanio**, **Gratiano**, **Solanio**, **officers**, and **clerks**, and finally, **the duke**.

DUKE: Well, is Antonio here?

ANTONIO: Ready, your honor.

DUKE: I am sorry for you. You have come
To answer a hard-hearted adversary,
An inhuman wretch incapable of pity,
Totally empty of even a drop of mercy!

ANTONIO: I shall meet his fury
With patience. I'm ready to suffer his rage
With a quietness of spirit.

DUKE: Go, someone,
And call the Jew into the court.

SOLANIO: He is already at the door.
He's coming, my lord.

DUKE: Make way for him,
And let him stand before me.

(The crowd parts and **Shylock** stands before the duke, bowing low.)

ACT 4
SCENE
1

Shylock, the world thinks—and so do I—
That you plan to keep up this malice only
Until the last minute. Then it's thought that
You will show mercy and remorse even
    stranger than this apparent cruelty.
And where you now demand the penalty,
    a pound of this poor merchant's flesh,
You will finally relent. Touched with
Human gentleness and love, you will even
Forgive part of the original debt. Some say
That you'll have pity because of the losses
That have recently fallen so heavily on him.
Such losses would cripple a royal merchant
And touch the hardest of hearts.

   (He pauses.)

We all expect a gentle answer, Shylock.

SHYLOCK: I have told your grace my plans.
I have sworn by our holy Sabbath to have
Full payment for default on my bond.
If you deny it, let the danger fall upon
Your city's constitution and freedom.
    You'll ask me why I choose to have
A pound of dead flesh rather than to receive

Three thousand ducats. I'll not answer that!
But say it is my whim! Is it answered?
What if my house is troubled with a rat,
And I am pleased to give 10,000 ducats
To have it poisoned? Is that answer good?
I won't give any other reason, apart from
the firm hatred that I have for Antonio,
For pursuing a losing battle with him.
Are you answered now?

BASSANIO: This is no answer, you unfeeling man, to
make excuses for your cruelty!

SHYLOCK: I am not obliged to please you
With my answers!

BASSANIO: Do all men kill the things
They do not love?

SHYLOCK: Wouldn't any man want
To kill the things he hates?

BASSANIO: Not every offense causes hate.

SHYLOCK: What—would you let a snake
Sting you twice?

ANTONIO *(to Bassanio):* You think you can
Reason with the Jew? You may as well

Go stand upon the beach and tell the tide
Not to reach its usual height.
Or you might as well ask the wolf why
He has made the ewe cry for its lamb.
You may as well forbid the mountain pines
To sway or to make a noise when they are
Buffeted by the winds. Anything that hard
You might as well try to do, as try to soften
that hardest thing of all—his heart.
Therefore, I beg you make no more offers,
Use no other methods. As soon as possible,
Let me know the court's decision,
And let the Jew have his will!

BASSANIO: I offer double your 3,000 ducats!

SHYLOCK: If every one of your 6,000 ducats
Were in six parts, and every part a ducat,
I would not take it. I demand my bond!

DUKE: How can you hope for mercy,
When you give none?

SHYLOCK: What judgment should I dread,
Having done no wrong? Many among you
Have slaves. You use them like your dogs

And mules—for wretched jobs, because
You bought them. Shall I say to you,
"Set them free. Marry them to your heirs.
Why should they sweat, carrying burdens?
Let their beds be as soft as yours, and
Their food as good." You would answer,

   "The slaves are ours." I say the same.
The pound of flesh which I demand of him
Is dearly bought. It is mine. I will have it.
If you deny me, I scorn your laws!
The decrees of Venice have no force.
I insist on justice. Answer! Shall I have it?

DUKE: I have the power to dismiss this court,
   Unless Bellario, a learned doctor of law,
   Whom I have sent for to resolve this case,
   Comes here today.

SOLANIO: My lord, a messenger has just come
   From Padua, with letters from the doctor.

DUKE: Bring me the letters.

BASSANIO: Cheer up, Antonio! Be brave!
   The Jew shall have my flesh, blood, bones,
   And all, before you shall lose
   One drop of blood for me.

(**Shylock** takes out a knife and begins to sharpen it on the soles of his leather shoes.)

ANTONIO: I am the weakest ram in the flock,
  Best suited for death. The weakest fruit
  Drops first to the ground, and so let me.
  You cannot be better used, Bassanio,
  Than to stay alive and write my epitaph.

(**Nerissa** enters, dressed as a judge's clerk.)

DUKE: Did you come from Bellario?

NERISSA: Yes. He sends his greetings.

(**She** presents a letter, which the **duke** reads.)

BASSANIO *(to Shylock)*: Why do you
  Sharpen your knife so earnestly?

SHYLOCK: To cut out my pound of flesh.

GRATIANO: You sharpen it not on your
  Shoe's sole but on your immortal soul!
  No metal, not even the executioner's axe,
  Is half as keen as your sharp envy.
  Can no prayers touch you?

SHYLOCK: None that you have brains to make.

GRATIANO: Damn you, you stubborn dog!
  Justice is to blame for letting you live.

I almost doubt my faith and share the theory

That the souls of animals can enter men.

Your spirit comes from a wolf whose soul,

When he was hanged for killing humans,

Fled into the womb of your unholy mother

And settled into you! Your desires

Are wolfish, bloody, mean, and hungry!

SHYLOCK: Until you can remove the seal from

My bond, you merely damage your lungs

To speak so loud. I'm here for justice.

DUKE: This letter from Bellario commends

A young and learned doctor of law

To our court. Where is he?

NERISSA: He is waiting nearby to hear

Your answer. Will you admit him?

DUKE: With all my heart. Three or four of you,

Go and escort him to this place.

(**Attendants** leave.)

Now, the court shall hear Bellario's letter.

(He reads.)

"Your grace, when your letter arrived, I was very

sick. But when your messenger came, a young

> doctor of law from Rome was visiting me. I
> told him of the lawsuit between Shylock and
> Antonio. We consulted many books together. I
> have asked him to come to you in my place.
> I beg you, do not underestimate him because of
> his lack of years. I never knew so young a body
> with so old a head.
> I trust you will accept him. His performance
> will speak for itself."

(He looks up.)

You hear what Bellario has written.

(**Portia** enters, dressed as a judge, carrying a lawbook.)

And here, I take it, is the doctor himself.

(He greets her.) Give me your hand.

(They shake.) You came from old Bellario?

PORTIA: I did, my lord.

DUKE: You are welcome. Take your place.

(A court usher guides **Portia** to a desk near the **duke**.)

Are you familiar with the case
Before the court?

PORTIA: Yes, I am.

Which is the merchant, and which the Jew?

DUKE: Antonio and Shylock, stand up.

PORTIA: Is your name Shylock?

SHYLOCK: Shylock is my name.

PORTIA: Your case is unusual.
But it is sound enough that Venetian laws
Cannot stop you from proceeding.
(to Antonio): You stand in some danger
From him, do you not?

ANTONIO: Yes, so he says.

PORTIA: Do you admit to the bond?

ANTONIO: I do.

PORTIA: Then the Jew must be merciful.

SHYLOCK: And what forces me to be? Tell me!

PORTIA: The quality of mercy is not strained.
It drops like a gentle rain from heaven
Upon the place beneath. It is twice blessed.
It blesses him that gives, and him that takes.
It is mightiest in the mightiest. It is more
becoming to the king than his crown.
His scepter shows his earthly power,
The symbol of his awe and majesty,

The reason kings are held in fear and dread.
   But mercy is above this sceptered rule.
It is enthroned in the hearts of kings.
It is a quality of God himself.
Earthly power is nearest to God's
When mercy balances justice. So, Jew—
Though you claim justice, consider this:
None of us could expect salvation if justice
Alone won out. We pray for mercy,
And that same prayer teaches us all to do

The deeds of mercy. I have said all this
　　to soften the justice of your pleas.
If you insist on it, this strict court of Venice
Has no choice but to pronounce sentence
Against the merchant there.

SHYLOCK: I'll answer for my own sins!
I want the law to enforce my bond!

PORTIA: Is he not able to pay the money?

BASSANIO: Yes, I offer it to him now in court.
It is twice the sum. If that is not enough,
I will pay ten times the amount,
On forfeit of my hands, my head, my heart!
If this is not enough, malice hides the truth.

(He kneels before **Portia** as if in prayer.)

I beg you: Twist the law your way.
To do a great right, do a little wrong, and
Stop this cruel devil from having his will!

PORTIA: That cannot be. No power in Venice
Can change a standing law. It would create
A precedent, and cause many errors
By the same example. It cannot be.

SHYLOCK: Oh, wise young judge, I honor you!

(He kisses the hem of her robe.)

PORTIA: Allow me to read the bond.

SHYLOCK *(handing it over)*: Here it is,
Most reverend doctor. Here it is!

PORTIA *(accepting the document without reading it)*:
Shylock, three times
Your money has been offered to you.

SHYLOCK: My oath! My oath!
I have vowed an oath to heaven!
Shall my soul be guilty of perjury?
No—not even for all of Venice!

PORTIA *(reading the bond)*: Why, this bond
Is forfeit. By this, the Jew may lawfully
Claim a pound of flesh, to be cut off by him
Nearest to the merchant's heart.
(to Shylock): Be merciful. Take three times
The money. Tell me to tear up the bond.

SHYLOCK: When it is paid according to the
Agreement. You appear to be a good judge.
You know the law. In the name of
The law, I demand judgment.

ANTONIO: I strongly beg the court
To give the judgment.

PORTIA *(to Antonio)*: Well, then, here it is:
　　You must prepare your breast for his knife.

SHYLOCK: Noble judge! Excellent young man!

PORTIA: The purpose of the law is to support
　　The penalty, which *(indicating the bond)*
　　Here seems due, according to the bond.

SHYLOCK: That's very true. Oh, wise judge!

PORTIA *(to Antonio)*: So, lay bare your breast.

SHYLOCK: Yes, his chest. So says the bond,
　　"Nearest his heart." The very words.

PORTIA: That's so. Are there scales here,
　　To weigh the flesh?

SHYLOCK: I have them ready.

(He opens his cloak to show them.)

PORTIA: Order a doctor to stand by, Shylock,
　　To stop his wounds
　　So he won't bleed to death.

SHYLOCK: Does it say that in the bond?

(He takes up the document and reads it.)

PORTIA: It is not spelled out, but what of that?
　　You'd do that much out of charity.

SHYLOCK: I can't find it. It's not in the bond.

(He hands back the document.)

PORTIA: Merchant, have you anything to say?

ANTONIO: Very little. I am well-prepared.
Give me your hand, Bassanio. Farewell.
   Don't grieve about this.
In my case, Fortune is kinder than usual.
Often she lets the wretched man outlive
His wealth, to endure with sunken eyes
And wrinkled brow an old age of poverty.
She has spared me that lingering misery.
Remember me to your honorable wife.
   Tell her how Antonio came to die,
And say how I loved you.
Speak well of me in death.
When the tale is told, ask her to judge
Whether or not Bassanio was loved.
   Only regret that you lose your friend
Who has no regret about paying your debt.
If the Jew cuts deep enough,
I'll pay it instantly, with all my heart!

BASSANIO: Antonio, I am married to a wife
Who is as dear to me as life itself.

But life itself, my wife, and all the world
Are not more precious to me than your life.
I would lose all—yes, sacrifice them all—
To save you!

PORTIA: Your wife would not thank you for
That, if she heard you make such an offer.

GRATIANO: I have a wife whom I swear I love.
I wish she were in heaven, so she could
Beg some power to change this Jew!

ACT 4
SCENE
1

NERISSA: It's well you say it behind her back.
That wish would make an unhappy house.

SHYLOCK *(aside)*: These Christian husbands!
I have a daughter. I'd rather she married
Anyone else besides a Christian!
(aloud) We're wasting time. I beg you,
Proceed to sentence.

PORTIA: A pound of that merchant's flesh
Is yours. The court awards it,
And the law permits it.

SHYLOCK: Most rightful judge!

PORTIA: You must cut it from his breast.
The law allows it, and the court awards it.

SHYLOCK: Most learned judge! A sentence!

(He moves with knife drawn toward **Antonio**.)

Come, prepare!

PORTIA: Wait a little. There's something else.
This bond gives you not one drop of blood.
The exact words are "a pound of flesh."
So you may take your bond and your pound of
flesh.
But, if in cutting it, you shed one drop of
Christian blood, your lands and goods,
Under the laws of Venice, will be
Confiscated to the state of Venice.

SHYLOCK *(appalled)*: Is that the law?

PORTIA *(opening the lawbook)*: You can see
For yourself. You pressed for justice.
Be assured you shall have even more
Justice than you want.

GRATIANO: Oh, learned judge!

SHYLOCK: I take the offer then. Pay
Three times the bond, and let him go.

BASSANIO: Here's the money.

PORTIA *(raising her hand)*: Gently now!
    The Jew shall have justice.
    He shall have nothing but the penalty.

GRATIANO: Oh, upright, learned judge!

PORTIA: Therefore, prepare to cut the flesh.
    Shed no blood. And cut neither less
    Nor more than exactly one pound of flesh.
    If you take more or less than one pound,
    Even if by one twentieth of an ounce—
    If the scale turns by so little as a hair—
    Then you shall die, and all your goods
    Will be confiscated.
    Why do you pause? Take your forfeit.

ACT 4 SCENE 1

SHYLOCK *(thwarted)*: Give me my money,
    And let me go.

BASSANIO: I have it ready for you. Here it is.

PORTIA: He has refused it in open court.
    He shall have strict justice and his bond.

SHYLOCK: Not even my money back?

PORTIA: You shall have nothing but the forfeit,
    And that to be taken at your peril, Jew.

SHYLOCK: I'll stand for no more of this!

(He turns to leave.)

PORTIA: Wait a moment, Jew.

The law has yet another hold on you.

(She consults the lawbook again.)

It is a law of Venice that if it is proved
Against an alien that he directly
Or indirectly seeks the life of any citizen,
The person against whom he plots
Can seize one half of his goods.
The other half goes to the state treasury.
The life of the offender lies only at the
Mercy of the duke.

(She closes the book.)

It appears from your actions that indirectly,
And directly too, you have plotted against
The very life of the defendant. You are
Indeed in danger of the death penalty.
Down on your knees, therefore,
And beg for the duke's mercy.

DUKE: To show the difference in our spirits,
I pardon your life before you ask for it.
Half your wealth goes to Antonio.
The other half goes to the state.
Your contrition could turn this to a fine.

PORTIA: Yes, the state's half. Not Antonio's.

SHYLOCK: No, take my life as well!
Don't pardon that. You take my house,
When you remove my source of income.
You take my life when you take away
The means by which I earn a living.

PORTIA: What mercy can you offer, Antonio?

ACT 4
SCENE 1

ANTONIO: I would be pleased if the court
Were willing to give up the state's half,
And let me have the other half to use
During his lifetime. After that, I'll give it
To the gentleman who recently eloped with
His daughter. Two more conditions.
  One: In exchange for this favor,
He shall become a Christian immediately.
Two: That he makes a will here in court,
Leaving all he possesses at his death
To his son-in-law Lorenzo and his daughter.

DUKE: Very well. He shall do this—or I will take
  back
The pardon that I have just pronounced!

PORTIA: Do you agree, Jew?

SHYLOCK: I agree.

PORTIA *(to Nerissa)*: Clerk, draw up a will.

SHYLOCK: Please, give me permission to go.
I am not well. Send the will after me,
And I will sign it.

DUKE: You may leave, but see you do it!

(**Shylock** exits, a broken man.)

Antonio, reward this young man.
I think you are greatly indebted to him.

(The **duke** and his **attendants** leave.)

BASSANIO *(to Portia)*: My good sir,
My friend and I have been spared
Grave penalties because of your wisdom.
We gladly give you the 3,000 ducats
That were due to the Jew.

ANTONIO: And, in love and gratitude,
We stand indebted to you
Far more than that, forevermore.

PORTIA *(refusing the money)*: He is well-paid
Who is well-satisfied. And in saving you,
I am satisfied. Therefore, I count myself
Well-paid. *(bowing)* Pray, remember me
When we meet again.

(She starts to leave.)

BASSANIO *(stopping her)*: Dear sir, I must
Ask you again to take some souvenir of us
As a gesture, not as a fee.
Grant me two things, I beg you.
Pardon my persistence, and don't say no.

PORTIA: You press me hard, so I'll give in.
Give me your gloves. I'll wear them
For your sake.

(**Bassanio** removes them.)

And, in token of your love,
I'll take this ring from you.

(**Bassanio** withdraws his hand sharply.)

Don't draw back your hand.
Surely you shall not deny me this?

BASSANIO: But this ring, good sir—
Alas, it is a trifle.
I would not shame myself to give it to you.

PORTIA: I will have nothing else but this ring.
I've taken a fancy to it.

BASSANIO: This ring is more important to me
Than its value. I will give you

The most valuable ring in Venice,

And I'll find it by advertising for it.

With respect, you must pardon me for this.

PORTIA: I see, sir, you are generous in offers.

First you taught me how to beg, and now

You teach me how a beggar

Should be answered.

BASSANIO: Good sir, this ring was given to me

By my wife. When she put it on my hand,

She made me vow that I should

Neither sell it, nor give it away, nor lose it.

PORTIA: That's an excuse many men use to

Keep their gifts. If your wife knew

How well I deserve this ring, she would

Not stay angry with you for giving

It to me. Well, peace be with you!

(**She** leaves, followed by **Nerissa**.)

ANTONIO *(distressed)*: Lord Bassanio,

Let him have the ring.

Weigh his worthiness and my love

Against your wife's commandment!

BASSANIO *(giving in)*: Go, Gratiano.
    Run and catch him. Give him the ring.
    Go quickly!

(**Gratiano** hurries off.)

    (to Antonio): Come. Let's go and rest.
    Early in the morning we'll go to Belmont.

(**They** leave together.)

ACT 4
SCENE 1

Scene ❷ 🎧

A street outside the law courts in Venice. **Portia** and **Nerissa** enter.

PORTIA *(giving a paper to Nerissa)*: Ask the way to
the Jew's house.
Give him this, and have him sign it.
We'll leave tonight and be home a day
Before our husbands get there.
Lorenzo will be glad to get this will.

(Gratiano enters, breathless from running.)

GRATIANO: Finally, I've caught up with you.
My Lord Bassanio has sent you this ring.

PORTIA: I accept his ring most thankfully.
Please tell him so. One more thing!
Please show my clerk old Shylock's house.

GRATIANO: I'll do that.

NERISSA *(to Portia)*: Sir, a word with you.
(She takes Portia aside.) I'll see if
I can get my husband's ring—the one
  he swore to keep forever!

ACT 4
SCENE 2

PORTIA: You can, I'm sure. No doubt they'll
Swear they gave the rings away to men!
But we'll stand up to them—
And outswear them, too. Now hurry!
You know where I'll be waiting.

(**Portia** leaves.)

NERISSA *(to Gratiano)*: Come, good sir.
Will you show me to his house?

(**They** leave in the direction of Shylock's house.)

ACT 5

Summary

在貝爾蒙，羅倫佐和潔西卡在波西亞的
花園中等待，此時大家也紛紛回來。有
好一陣子，波西亞和奈莉莎兩人用戒指的事情捉弄她們的
丈夫。兩位男士堅稱他們實在無計可施，是被迫放棄戒指
的。當真相大白時，大家都笑了，誓言將永遠愛著彼此，並
手挽著手進到屋子裡。

Scene ❶ 🎧

Lorenzo and Jessica are in the garden of Portia's house in Belmont. It is a moonlit summer night. Stephano, Portia's servant, comes running up, followed by Lancelot, Bassanio's servant.

STEPHANO: Hello! Where's Master Lorenzo?

LORENZO: Stop yelling, man! Here I am.

STEPHANO: A messenger has come with
News. My mistress will be here by morning.

LANCELOT: And my master is also on his way.

(Lancelot leaves.)

LORENZO: Dearest, let's go in and prepare
For their arrival. And yet—why?
Why should we go in?
(to Stephano): My friend Stephano, please tell
those
In the house that your mistress is nearby,
And then bring the musicians out.

(Stephano goes indoors.)

How sweetly the moonlight sleeps here!
We will sit, and let the sounds of music
Fall gently on our ears. Look, Jessica,

See how the night sky is dotted

With tiles of bright gold. Even the smallest

Star sings in his movements

Like an angel sings in a choir.

Such harmony is also in immortal souls.

But while we are in our mortal bodies,

We cannot hear it.

(**Musicians** come out and disappear among the trees.
Lorenzo calls out to them.)

Begin, then. With soft chords,

Reach your mistress's ear,

And draw her home with music.

(to Jessica): Listen to the music!

(Music plays. **Portia** and **Nerissa** enter.)

PORTIA *(looking toward the house)*: That light

We see is burning in my hallway.

How far that little candle throws its beams!

So shines a good deed in a wicked world.

NERISSA: When the moon shone,

We didn't see the candle.

PORTIA: That's because greater powers

Dim the lesser. A stand-in looks as regal

As a king until the real king comes by.

Then his importance lessens, like an
Inland brook does when it reaches the sea.
(She listens.) Music! Listen!

NERISSA: They are your own musicians,
Coming from your house.

PORTIA: How important the setting is!
I think it sounds much sweeter than by day.

NERISSA: The silence improves it, madam.

PORTIA: The crow sings as sweetly as the lark
When no one is listening. If a nightingale
Sang by day, when every barnyard fowl
Is cackling, would it be thought
  no better a musician than the wren?
How many things sound better
In the right season and at the right time!
Quiet now! The moon rests behind a cloud,
And does not want to be awakened.

(The music stops as the light fades.)

LORENZO: Oh! That is the voice—
Or I am much mistaken—of Portia!

PORTIA: You know me as the blind man
Knows the cuckoo—by the bad voice.

LORENZO: Dear lady, welcome home!

PORTIA: We've been praying for the welfare
Of our husbands. Have they returned yet?

LORENZO: No, madam, not yet.
But a messenger said they are on their way.

PORTIA: Go in, Nerissa. Tell my servants
Not to mention that we were gone.
Nor must you, Lorenzo. Jessica, nor you!

(A trumpet sounds, announcing **Bassanio**.)

LORENZO: Your husband is nearby. *(winking)*
We are not telltales, madam. Fear not.

(The cloud passes by. The scene is moonlit again.)

PORTIA: This night seems more like daylight
When it is sick. It looks a little paler—
Like a day when the sun is hidden.

(**Bassanio**, **Antonio**, **Gratiano**, and their **followers** arrive. **Gratiano** and **Nerissa** stand aside and talk separately.)

PORTIA: Welcome home, my lord.

BASSANIO: Thank you, madam.
Welcome my friend, too. Here is the man—
This is Antonio—to whom I owe so much.

PORTIA: You should feel deeply honored.

I hear he nearly paid a great debt for you.

ANTONIO: No more than I was glad to pay.

PORTIA: You are very welcome to our home.

GRATIANO *(to Nerissa, as they have been arguing about the ring)*: By the moon above,

I swear you are wrong! Honestly,

I gave it to the judge's clerk.

May he lose his manhood for all I care,

Since you take it so much to heart, my love!

PORTIA *(overhearing)*: A quarrel already?

What's the matter?

GRATIANO: It's about a hoop of gold,

A paltry ring she gave me. It had words

Engraved on it: "Love me. Leave me not."

NERISSA: Why talk about the words on it

Or the value of it? You swore to

Wear it until the hour of your death! You

Said it would lie with you in your grave.

For the sake of your passionate oaths,

You should have kept it.

Gave it to a judge's clerk! How well I know

That the clerk will never have a beard!

GRATIANO: He will, if he lives to be a man.

NERISSA: Yes, if a woman lives to be a man!

GRATIANO: On my honor! I gave it to a youth,
A kind of boy. A little, well-scrubbed boy,
No taller than you. He begged it as a fee.
I could not for all my heart deny it to him.

PORTIA: You were to blame. I must be frank.
To part so lightly with your wife's first gift!
I gave my love a ring, and made him swear
Never to part with it, and here he stands—

I'll vouch that he would not leave it,

Or pull it from his finger, for all the wealth

In the world. Now truly, Gratiano,

You've caused your wife some grief,

And if it were me, I'd be angry about it.

BASSANIO *(aside)*: I'd better cut my left hand

Off and swear I lost the ring defending it.

GRATIANO: Lord Bassanio gave his ring to the

Judge who begged it from him. He

Indeed deserved it, too. Then his clerk,

Who took so much trouble with the papers,

Begged for mine. Neither clerk nor

Judge would take anything but the rings.

PORTIA: Which ring did you give, my lord?

Not the one you got from me, I hope.

BASSANIO: If I could add a lie to a fault,

I would deny it. But you can see my finger

Does not have the ring on it. It is gone.

PORTIA *(turning away)*: And your false heart

Is just as empty of the truth! By heaven,

I will not sleep with you until I see the ring.

NERISSA *(to Gratiano)*: Nor will I sleep with you,
  Gratiano, until I see my ring again.

BASSANIO: Sweet Portia! If you knew
  To whom, for whom, and why I gave it,
  You wouldn't be so angry!

PORTIA: If you had known the ring's meaning,
  Or half the worthiness of she who gave it,
  Or your own duty to keep it,
  You would never have parted with it!
  No man would be so unreasonable as to
  Insist on an item of such sentimental value.
  Nerissa has the right idea. Upon my life,
  Some woman has that ring!

BASSANIO: On my honor, madam, no woman
  Has it. I gave it to a judge who refused
  3,000 ducats from me and begged
  For the ring. At first, I denied him—
  Even though he had saved the very life of
  My dear friend! Sweet lady, what can I say?
  I was forced to send it after him.
  Filled with shame, I owed him a courtesy.
    My honor would not be smeared

118

By such ingratitude. Pardon me, good lady.
By all these stars, if you had been there,
I think you would have begged me to
Give the ring to the worthy judge.

PORTIA: Let that judge never come near me!
But since he has the jewel that I loved
And that you swore to keep for me,
I will be as generous as you.
I'll not deny him anything I have—
Not my body nor my husband's bed.
I shall know him, I am sure of it.
If I'm left alone, by my honor—
Which is mine to give—I'll have that
Judge for a bedfellow!

NERISSA: And I'll have his clerk! Therefore,
Be careful not to leave me alone!

GRATIANO: Well, go on then. But don't let me
Catch him, for if I do, I'll—

ANTONIO *(interrupting)*: How sad that I am the
Unhappy subject of these quarrels.

PORTIA: Please, sir, don't you worry.
You are welcome anyway.

ACT 5
SCENE
1

119

BASSANIO: Portia, forgive me this wrong,
Which was forced on me. With our friends
As witnesses, I swear to you that
I will never break another oath!

ANTONIO: I once loaned my body to obtain
His happiness. But if not for the man
Who has your ring, I'd have lost my life.
Now I'll dare to be the guarantor again,
With my soul as forfeit,
I swear that your husband
Will never again break faith with you.

PORTIA: Then you shall be his guarantor.
(taking off the ring) Give him this,
And tell him to keep it better than the other.

ANTONIO: Here, Lord Bassanio,
Swear to keep this ring.

BASSANIO: By heaven, it is the same one
I gave to the judge.

PORTIA: I got it from him.
Forgive me, Bassanio. In return
For this ring, the judge slept with me.

NERISSA *(also showing a ring)*: And
    Forgive me, gentle Gratiano.
    That boy, the judge's clerk, lay with me
    Last night on payment of this ring.

GRATIANO: What—are our wives unfaithful
    Before we have deserved it?

PORTIA: Don't speak so grossly.
    (She decides to explain.) Here is a letter.
    It's from Bellario in Padua.
    In it you will learn that
    Portia was the judge and Nerissa her clerk.
    Lorenzo can say that I left soon after you,
    And just now returned. I have not yet
    Entered my house. Antonio, welcome!
    I have better news in store for you
    Than you expect. *(She produces another letter.)*
    Read this. It says that three of your
    Ships unexpectedly reached safe harbor.
    How I stumbled on this letter is a secret.

ANTONIO: What? I'm speechless!

BASSANIO *(to Portia)*: Were you the judge,
    And I didn't know you?

GRATIANO *(to Nerissa)*: Were you the clerk
    Who fancied an affair behind my back?

NERISSA: Yes, but the clerk never means to
    Do it—unless he lives to be a man!

BASSANIO *(to Portia)*: Sweet judge,
    You shall sleep with me! And when
    I am away, then sleep with my wife.

ANTONIO *(after reading his letter)*:
    Sweet lady, you have given me life
    And a future. For now I know for certain
    That my ships have safely come to port.

PORTIA: Well, now, Lorenzo,
    My clerk has good news for you, too.

NERISSA: And I'll give it to him without a fee.
(She hands over the will she has prepared.)
    Here I give to you and Jessica a special
    Deed of gift from the rich Jew.
    Upon his death, you will have all he owns.

LORENZO: Fair ladies, you drop manna—
    Food from heaven—before starving people!

PORTIA: It is almost morning.
    I'm sure you haven't got the whole story.

Let us go in. You can ask questions there,
And we will answer all things honestly.

GRATIANO: Let's do that. The first question
That my Nerissa must answer is this:
Would she rather wait until tomorrow night
Or go to bed now, when there are
Only two more hours until daylight?
If it were day, I would wish it dark,
So I'd be sleeping with the judge's clerk.
While I live, nothing will worry me more
Than the safekeeping of Nerissa's ring!

(They **all** enter the house, arm in arm.)

中文翻譯

背景
英文內文 P. 004

巴薩尼歐為了向女繼承人波西亞求婚，向他的友人安東尼歐借錢。安東尼歐向一名猶太高利貸業者夏洛克借錢。

因為夏洛克痛恨所有基督徒，尤其是安東尼歐，他捨棄平常會收的利息錢，反而要求安東尼歐，如果他在三個月內還不出錢的話，要收取一磅他的肉。隨後，安東尼歐的生意走下坡，他賠光了所有的錢，因而無法償還欠夏洛克的債務。

現在，因為女兒和一個基督徒私奔而對他們更為惱怒的夏洛克，向安東尼歐索取他的那一磅肉。一切看來都無望了，直到波西亞在法庭上現身，打扮成法官的模樣。她能聰明到做出公平的判決，因而救可憐的安東尼歐一命嗎？

人物介紹
P. 005

威尼斯公爵、摩洛哥親王和亞拉岡親王：波西亞的追求者
安東尼歐：威尼斯商人
巴薩尼歐：安東尼歐的朋友
格拉西安諾、索拉尼歐和撒萊利歐：安東尼歐和巴薩尼歐的
　朋友

羅倫佐：與潔西卡相戀

夏洛克：猶太高利貸業者

杜巴：另一位猶太人，夏洛克的朋友

朗西洛特・高波：夏洛克的僕人，後轉而服侍巴薩尼歐

老高波：朗西洛特的父親

李奧納多：巴薩尼歐的僕人

巴爾薩澤和史迪凡諾：波西亞的僕人

波西亞：貝爾蒙的富家女

奈莉莎：波西亞的侍女

潔西卡：夏洛克的女兒

法庭官員、獄卒、僕人和隨從

第一幕

●第一場 ——————————————— P. 007

（十六世紀義大利威尼斯的一處碼頭；安東尼歐正和朋友索拉尼歐
及撒萊利歐說話。）

安東尼歐（嘆氣）：我不知道我為什麼這麼悲傷，這種情緒讓我
　　厭煩，你說它也讓你厭煩。但我如何染上、發現或得到這種
　　情緒，我不知道。我覺得非常悲傷，甚至快不認識自己了。

撒萊利歐：你的心思正隨大海翻滾。（指著大海。）它在那裡，
　　你的船隻鼓起船帆，對著一般商船頤指氣使呢。

索拉尼歐：相信我，如果我要冒你那種風險，我也會煩惱。
　　任何讓我的投資有風險的事，都會讓我悲傷。

撒萊利歐：當我想到海上的強風可能會造成什麼災害，把我
　　的熱湯吹涼的一口氣，都會讓我著涼。當我看著沙漏裡的

沙，我就會想到淺海和沙岸，並看到我的其中一艘船陷在沙裡。每次我去教堂，聖石都會讓我想到危險的礁岩。它們只需要碰一下我那脆

弱的船隻，就會把她的香料灑到海裡，並讓那湍急的海水穿上我的絲綢！這一刻我很富有，下一刻我就一無所有。我將會多麼悲慘，如果這種事發生！你騙不了我，我知道安東尼歐一定是在擔心他的貨物。

安東尼歐：相信我，事情並不是這樣。我很幸運，我的投資並不是都在同一艘船上，或在同一個地方。我的錢財目前也並未全部遭受危險。因此，我的貨物並不是造成我悲傷的原因。

索拉尼歐（取笑）：那麼，你一定是戀愛了！

安東尼歐（抗議）：沒有的事！

索拉尼歐：也不是戀愛？那麼，我們假定，你悲傷是因為你不快樂。而如果你想要，你也可以開懷大笑的。（巴薩尼歐、羅倫佐和格拉西安諾上。）你高貴的親屬巴薩尼歐來了，格拉西安諾與羅倫佐和他一起來。（看到他離開的良機。）再會！現在，我們將你留給更好的同伴相陪。

撒萊利歐（也看到他的良機）：如果不是有更適合的同伴出現，我原要留下來讓你振作起來再走。

安東尼歐：你們人真好，但我想是你們自己有生意要辦，這給了你們離開的機會。

撒萊利歐（對新來者）：早安！

巴薩尼歐（熱情地）：兩位好！我們何時要歡聚呢？你們都快變陌生人了！一定要走嗎？

撒萊利歐（急著要離開）：好的，好的。我們這幾天找一天聚聚。
（撒萊利歐和索拉尼歐下。）

羅倫佐：巴薩尼歐，既然你現在已找到安東尼歐，我們就先走了，別忘了我們的晚餐之約。

巴薩尼歐：我一定會到！

格拉西安諾：你看起來臉色不好，安東尼歐。你讓生意把你弄得心情低落。別這麼煩惱。相信我，你最近都不像你了。

安東尼歐：我接受世界的原貌，格拉西安諾，是一個舞台，每個人都一定有個角色，而我的是個悲傷的角色。

格拉西安諾：那麼，讓我扮演小丑吧。讓歡樂與笑聲使我長出皺紋，讓我的情緒因酒而激昂，而不是讓我的心因嘆息而冷卻。為什麼一個熱血的男子，竟然成了如他祖父的冰冷石像一般？我告訴你，安東尼歐——而且我是出於友情而說——有些人的表情永遠不變。他們保持靜默，希望被視為有智慧、莊嚴且重要的人。安東尼歐，我認識有些人，他們的智慧名聲是得自於閉口不言。我很確定，如果他們開口，就會證明自己是傻瓜。這方面，我改天再跟你多說一點。但別用憂鬱當餌，來釣這種虛假的名聲，羅倫佐。（對安東尼歐：）現在，再會了。我晚餐後再來結束我的演講。

羅倫佐：是的，我們晚餐時再與你們相見。我一定是那種沈默的智者之一，因為格拉西安諾從不讓我說話。

格拉西安諾：再和我當兩年朋友——你就會忘記你自己的聲音！

安東尼歐（對格拉西安諾）：那麼，我猜想我最好開始說話。

格拉西安諾：悉聽尊便，沈默只在乾牛舌和年輕女子身上有好處！

（格拉西安諾和羅倫佐下。）

安東尼歐：你認為那話是什麼意思？

巴薩尼歐（大笑）：他說的廢話比威尼斯任何人都多！格拉西安諾說的任何真話，就像藏在兩大桶雜物裡的兩粒麥子。花了整天去找，等你找到，又覺得不值得花那個功夫了！

安東尼歐：那麼，現在，告訴我。你愛戀的那位小姐是誰？你答應今天會告訴我的。

巴薩尼歐（現在嚴肅起來）：安東尼歐，你很清楚我一直入不敷出地揮霍著遺產。我並不因為得節衣縮食而生氣，但我的主要目標，是要償還我的奢侈生活讓我欠下的大筆債務。我欠你最多，安東尼歐，金錢和友情都是。因為我們是朋友，我才敢毫無顧忌地說出我欲清償所有債務的計畫。

安東尼歐：巴薩尼歐，告訴我一切。如果你的計畫是正直的
——就像你一樣——那麼，我保證我的錢包、我的人和我
所有的資源都為你所用。

巴薩尼歐：我念書的時候，如果我遺失了一支箭，我就朝同一
個方向再射一支。我仔細看著它的飛行路線，以找出第一
支箭落在哪裡。藉由冒著失去兩支箭的風險，我通常兩支
都能找到。我說出這個童年故事，是因為我的新計畫很類
似。我欠你許多錢——全怪我年輕——而且把欠的錢也丟
了。但如果你願意朝第一箭的方向再射一箭，我要不是能
找到兩支箭，就是能把第二支箭再拿回來還給你。然後，
我會滿懷感激地謹記欠你的第一筆債務。

安東尼歐：你認識我夠深了。懷疑我是否會幫助你，比你把
我所有的財產都花光還傷我更深。只管告訴我要怎麼做，
然後我就去做！

巴薩尼歐：在貝爾蒙有位富有的女繼承人。她美麗而端莊。
有時，我會收到她眼神散發出的無聲訊息。她的名字是波
西亞。世人並未忽略她的價值，因為四面八方的風，從每
個海岸吹來有名的追求者。安東尼歐，只要我有錢和這些
追求者一較高下，我確信我可以求婚成功。

安東尼歐：你知道我的財產都繫於海上的貨物。我沒有現
金，目前也沒有任何東西可變賣。因此，去威尼斯，看看
我的信用能發揮什麼作用。盡量利用它來資助你的貝爾
蒙之旅，去見美麗的波西亞。現在就去，四處打聽，我也
是。看看哪裡有錢可以取得。用我的信用和好名聲借錢。
不管哪一種，結果都是要借到錢。

（巴薩尼歐和安東尼歐下。）

●第二場

（波西亞於貝爾蒙住家的大廳；波西亞正和她的侍女奈莉莎說話。）

波西亞：說實話，奈莉莎，我小小的身軀厭煩了這個廣大的世界。

奈莉莎：如果你的不幸和你的好運一樣多，親愛的小姐，你會覺得比較富裕。我的看法是，擁有太多的人和擁有太少的人一樣悲慘。過量會帶給你白髮並讓你未老先衰！中庸才會讓人活得久。

波西亞：好句子，而且說得好。

奈莉莎：如果好好遵循會更好。

波西亞：如果行動和知道要做什麼一樣容易，那麼窮人的小屋就會變成宮殿了。一個好傳教士會遵循自己的教誨。我寧願教導二十個人如何行事，也不願是遵循我自己教誨的那二十個人之一！大腦可能會試圖控制情緒，但急躁的脾氣會跳過冷酷的規矩。年輕人無視有益的忠告，因為那是種阻礙。但這些道理都無助我選擇丈夫。喔，天啊！（嘆氣。）「選擇」那個詞！我可能既無法選擇我喜歡的人，也無法拒絕我不喜歡的人。在世的女兒的意願受限於已逝父親的意願。奈莉莎，這不是很不公平嗎？因為我既無法選擇也無法拒絕。

奈莉莎：您的父親品德非常高尚，而且好人在臨終時常受到啟發。他設下的抽籤方式是很相稱的辦法。從金、銀或鉛中選擇——而你是作出正確選擇的獎品——有適合你的男子才會選對。你對那些已經前來求婚的親王們感覺如何？

波西亞：請說出他們的名字。在你說的時候，我可以把他們形容給你聽。然後，你可以從我的形容中，猜出我對他們每個人的感覺。

奈莉莎：首先是那不勒斯親王。

波西亞：喔，是的，那匹小雄馬！他除了談他的馬，其他什麼
　　　也不做。他自誇，他可以自己為馬釘蹄鐵。我懷疑，他的
　　　母親曾和鐵匠有染！

奈莉莎：然後是那位有王權的伯爵。

波西亞：他除了皺眉，什麼也不做，彷彿在說：「如果你不想
　　　嫁給我，就選別人吧！」他聽笑話從來不笑。我確信，等
　　　他年老會成為哭泣的先知，因為年輕時就滿懷著悲傷。我
　　　寧願嫁給骷髏，也不願嫁給這兩個其中一個！

奈莉莎：你覺得法國貴族勒邦先生如何呢？

波西亞：老實說，我知道嘲笑別人是種罪──但他不算！如
　　　果他恨我，我會很高興，因為我永遠無法回應他的愛。

奈莉莎：那位年輕的英國男爵呢？

波西亞：你知道，我從來沒和他說過話。他不了解我，我也不
　　　了解他。他既不會說拉丁文、法文，也不會說義大利文，而
　　　你知道，我的英文不好。他看起來很有男子氣概──但誰
　　　能和啞吧交談？還有他的打扮多怪異啊！我想，他的背心
　　　是在義大利買的，長襪在法國買的，帽子在德國買的，而
　　　他的行為舉止則學自世界各處！

奈莉莎：那位年輕的德國人呢？

波西亞：當他早上清醒時，我不喜歡他，當他下午喝醉時，我
　　　憎恨他。當他處於最佳狀態時，還稱不上是個人。當他處
　　　於最壞狀態時，他比一隻野獸好不到哪裡去。

奈莉莎：如果他要求選擇並且選中正確的箱子怎麼辦？如果
　　　你拒絕與他成婚，你就違背了你父親的意願。

波西亞：因此，為了防止最糟的狀況發生，我要你把一大杯萊
　　　茵葡萄酒放在錯誤的箱子上面。就算裡面藏著惡魔，他也

會被引誘去選擇那個箱子。我什麼都願意做，奈莉莎，也不要嫁給醉鬼！

奈莉莎：親愛的小姐，你不需要擔心要嫁給這些貴族的任何一人。他們已經告訴我他們的決定了。除非他們能用你父親所設計的箱子選項以外的方法得到你，否則他們就要返回他們的家鄉，並且不再來煩你。

波西亞：除非有人能依照我父親的意願追求到我，否則我就以貞潔之身死去！我很高興這些追求者這麼明理。他們沒有一個人的缺席，會讓我不高興的。

奈莉莎：你還記得，小姐，有位威尼斯來的追求者嗎？

波西亞：是的，記得！是巴薩尼歐。至少，我想那是他的名字。

奈莉莎：沒錯，小姐。我這愚蠢的雙眼所見過的所有男人中，他是最能配上美麗淑女的一個。

波西亞：我清楚記得他。是的，巴薩尼歐配得上你的讚美。（一名僕人上。）有什麼事？

僕人：有四位陌生人找你，小姐，要和你道別。一名來自第五人的信差剛到──來自摩洛哥親王。他宣布親王今晚會抵達。

波西亞：如果我能如同向那四位道別那樣熱情地迎接這第五位，我會很高興見他。來吧，奈莉莎。（對僕人：）帶路吧。（嘆氣。）我們才對一位追求者關上大門，另一人就來敲門！

（眾人下。）

●第三場 —————————————— P. 021

（威尼斯街道，夏洛克住家外；巴薩尼歐和夏洛克在討論借款的事。）

夏洛克：你想要三千元……。

巴薩尼歐：是的，先生。借三個月，安東尼歐會當保人。你願意借嗎？

夏洛克（大聲思考）：三千元借三個月。安東尼歐要擔保……。

巴薩尼歐：你覺得如何？

夏洛克：安東尼歐是個好人。

巴薩尼歐：你有聽到不同的看法嗎？

夏洛克（大笑）：喔，不，不，不，不是！當我說「是個好人」，你得了解，我的意思是他在金錢方面很有信用。但他的財富現在有危險，他的商船正開往的黎波里、西印度群島、墨西哥和英格蘭──加上其他國外的風險。但船隻只是木頭，水手只是凡人。有旱老鼠和水老鼠，陸地盜賊和海上盜賊。我是指，海盜。然後，還有海洋、強風和礁岩的危險！即使如此，這個男人的根基還是很深厚的。你說三千元嗎？我想我可以借你。

巴薩尼歐：要確定你可以。

夏洛克：我會的。關於安東尼歐的生意，有什麼最新消息？來的這人是誰啊？

（安東尼歐上。）

巴薩尼歐：是安東尼歐。

夏洛克（竊語）：他看起來像個諂媚的客棧老闆！我痛恨他，因為他是基督徒。但他謙恭不收利息地把錢借出去，把威尼斯這裡的利率拉低了，這點讓我更加痛恨他。如果我可以神不知鬼不覺地逮到他的小辮子，我就可以好好報一箭之仇。他痛恨我們猶太人。他公開詆毀我這個人、我的生意，還有我辛苦賺來的利潤，他稱之為「放高利貸」。如果我饒過他，願我的族人遭到詛咒！

巴薩尼歐：夏洛克，你有在聽嗎？

夏洛克：我正在計算我的資產。就我最近的記憶所及，我沒辦法立刻湊足三千元。但那有什麼關係？杜巴，一位富有的猶太同胞會幫我的忙。但是，等等，我忘了——你打算什麼時候還錢？（向安東尼歐鞠躬。）別擔心，先生，我們剛剛才談到你。

安東尼歐：夏洛克，雖然我從來沒有在借出或借入金錢時，索取或付出高利，但我願為幫我的朋友而破例。（對巴薩尼歐：）他知道你要借多少嗎？

夏洛克：知道，知道，三千元。

安東尼歐：借三個月。

夏洛克：我倒忘了。對，三個月。你告訴過我。那麼，你的保人……我看看……。但聽著，我以為你說過，你從來沒有為了賺錢而借出或借入金錢。

安東尼歐：我從來沒有。

夏洛克：當雅各為他舅父拉班牧羊時——

安東尼歐（不耐地）：他怎麼了？他收了利息？

夏洛克：不，他沒收，不是你所謂的直接收利息。雅各是這麼做的。雅各和拉班說好，所有生下來有條紋和斑點的小羊都歸雅各所有，當作他的薪資。當母羊和公羊在交配時，這位有經驗的牧羊人就削好一些棍子，立在母羊眼前。此時，母羊懷孕了。因此，在生小羊時，牠們就會產下有條紋和其他斑點的小羊。那些小羊就歸雅各所有。這是一種獲利的方法，而且他是受到祝福的。利潤是種恩賜，如果人類不竊取的話。

安東尼歐：雅各做的是投機生意。（*嘲笑夏洛克的無知。*）棍子和生下的小羊一點關係也沒有。你告訴我們這個故事，是為了證明獲利的正當性嗎？還是你要聲稱，你的金子和銀子就是母羊和公羊？

夏洛克：我不能說，我讓它一樣快速地繁殖！

安東尼歐：注意了，巴薩尼歐。魔鬼會為了他自己的意圖而引述《聖經》文句。一個邪惡的人引述《聖經》，就像有著笑臉的惡棍，或是一顆果核已爛掉的漂亮蘋果。喔，虛假看起來是多麼吸引人啊！那麼，夏洛克，借錢的事怎麼說？

夏洛克：安東尼歐，你多次指責我的放貸業務。我都是聳聳肩忍下來，因為苦難正是我們族人的徽章。你叫我是異教徒，是割喉的狗，並對著我的猶太服裝吐口水，全都因為我使用我自己的財產！現在，顯然你需要我的幫助。你來找我，然後你說：「夏洛克，我們想要些錢。」你，曾對著我的鬍子吐口水，並像把一條野狗踢出你家一樣地踢我！我應該對你說什麼呢？「狗會有錢嗎？狗可能有三千元借你嗎？」還是我應該深深鞠躬，然後低聲下氣地說：「親愛的先生，你上星期三吐我口水；你某天某日把我一腳踢開；另外某次，你叫我是狗。因為這樣，我會借給你這麼多錢？」

安東尼歐：我很可能會再次這麼叫你，也會再吐你口水和踢你！如果你願意借出這筆錢，別好似借給朋友那般。什麼樣的友情，會要賺朋友的錢？而是，當作借給你的敵人。如果他還不出錢來，你可以更有立場地強力要求罰款。

夏洛克：看看你發多大的脾氣啊！我想要當朋友，要你愛我，忘掉你可恥的行為，並提供你所需的金錢，而且不收一毛利息。我向你釋出善意……。

巴薩尼歐：好個善意！

夏洛克：這是我要展示的善意。和我一起去見律師，簽一份協議書，而且——為了好玩——如果你未如約定還我錢，把罰金定為你的一磅肉，從你身體任何我喜歡的部位割下。

巴薩尼歐（對安東尼歐）：你不該為了我簽這樣的合約！沒有錢，我也會想出辦法的。

安東尼歐：喔，別擔心，老兄！兩個月內——那還提前一個月——我預期會有九倍於這合約的獲利。

夏洛克：喔，先祖亞伯拉罕！這些基督徒！他們自己愛計較的行為，讓他們誰都不信任。告訴我，如果他還不出錢，這張合約能讓我得到什麼？一磅人肉，還不如羊肉、牛肉或山羊肉有價值。我提出這樣的友好舉動，只為搏取他的善意。如果他接受，很好。如果不接受，再會。但別誤解了我。

安東尼歐：好的，夏洛克，我會簽合約。

夏洛克：那麼，到律師那裡和我碰面。現在，我要進去裡面，把錢湊齊。我很快就來。

（夏洛克進他家裡去。）

巴薩尼歐：我不相信出自一個惡棍的公平合約。

安東尼歐：來吧，沒什麼好驚慌的。我的船在期限前的一個月就會返回了。

（他們一起下。）

第二幕

● 第一場────────────── P. 031

（波西亞在貝爾蒙的家；摩洛哥親王及隨從上；波西亞、奈莉莎及僕
人等待訪客。）

摩洛哥：別因為我的膚色而不喜歡我。我的黝黑膚色是件制
服，由那些生活在燃燒黃銅太陽下的族群所穿。給我一位
來自北方最英俊的男子，那裡的太陽幾乎連一根冰柱都融
化不了。然後，叫我們兩人為你的愛之故，把我們的皮膚
割開，以證明誰的血最紅，他的還是我的。我告訴你，小
姐，我的這張臉曾嚇退過最勇敢的人。但我發誓，我們那
裡最美麗動人的女士也愛著它。我不會改變我的膚色，除
非是為了贏得你的關注，溫柔的女王。

波西亞：說到選擇，我不會只被外貌牽著鼻子走。再說，我父
親的意願不允許我選擇自己的命運。如果我父親未立下這
些條件，您，聲名遠播的王子，便和我到目前為止所見，
想贏得我的愛情的任何人有同樣的機會。

摩洛哥：感謝你的這番話。因此，請帶我去選箱子，這樣我
才能試試我的運氣。為了贏得你的愛，我會以目光壓倒最
嚴厲的雙眼，從母熊身邊搶走小熊，甚至嘲笑怒吼的雄
獅。但是，唉，如果兩名冠軍要以擲骰子決定誰比較偉
大，運氣可能會給較弱的一方較高的分數。因此，盲目的
運氣可能會導致我失去較弱的男子會得到的東西，然後我
會悲痛而亡。

波西亞：你得孤注一擲。你若非完全不選擇，就是得在選擇
前發誓，如果你選錯了，此後再也不能向任何女士求婚。
因此，請謹慎思考。

摩洛哥：我同意這條件。我願碰運氣。

波西亞：你得先到神殿，立下你的誓言。晚餐後，你就能冒險一試了。

摩洛哥：那麼，祝我好運！我要不是世上最幸福之人，就是受到最大詛咒之人。

（眾人下。）

●第二場 —————————————————— P. 034

（夏洛克家前面的街道。夏洛克的僕人朗西洛特高波上，撞到父親老高波，他已幾近全盲，提著一只籃子。）

老高波：少爺，請幫個忙。去猶太老爺家的路是哪一條？

朗西洛特（竊語）：喔，天啊！這是我的親生父親！幾近全盲的他，認不出我了。我且來戲弄他一下。（對老高波：）在下個路口右轉，但在下一個路口要左轉。到了再下一個路口，都不要轉，順著彎曲的路走下去，就會到猶太人家了！

老高波：聖人在上，那路真難走。你可以告訴我朗西洛特是否還住在他家？

朗西洛特（決定說出他的身分）：你認不得我了嗎，父親？

老高波：唉呀，我幾乎要瞎了，我認不出來。

朗西洛特：就算你沒瞎，你可能也認不得我。能認得自己孩子的父親是有智慧的。嗯，老頭，我有你兒子的消息要告訴你。我是朗西洛特，以前是你兒子，現在是你兒子，以後也會是你兒子。

老高波：我不敢相信你是我兒子！

朗西洛特：我不知要如何回應，但我是朗西洛特，而且我確定瑪格莉，你的妻子，是我母親。

老高波：她的名字的確是瑪格莉。那麼，如果你是朗西洛特，我發誓你就是我的骨肉。天啊，你變了好多！你和你家老爺處得好嗎？我帶了一個禮物要送他。

朗西洛特：我已經決定要逃走。送他禮物？送他個絞索吧！他讓我餓肚子。我的肋骨像手指一樣根根分明。（他拉著老高波的手摸他的肋骨。）父親，我很高興你來了。把這份禮物送給巴薩尼歐老爺吧。他真的提供很漂亮的制服呢！我要不是去服侍他，就是繼續逃亡。看！他來了。過去找他，父親。如果我再服侍猶太人，就唾棄我吧！

（巴薩尼歐和李奧納多及其他人上。）

巴薩尼歐（對一名僕人）：是的，但要趕快辦。我要晚餐在五點前準備好，把這幾封信送出去，給僕人訂新制服。然後，請格拉西安諾來我家。

（僕人下。）

朗西洛特：去找他，父親！

老高波（鞠躬）：閣下！

巴薩尼歐：有什麼事嗎？

老高波：這是我兒子，可憐的孩子——

朗西洛特（走向前）：不是可憐的孩子，先生，而是有錢猶太人的僕人，他想要的，我父親會告訴你——

（他躲在他父親身後。）

老高波：他想要，先生，服侍——

朗西洛特（再走向前）：嗯，長話短說是，我服侍猶太人，但我想轉而服侍你。

巴薩尼歐：我很清楚你的為人。這份工作是你的了。和你的舊東家道別，然後去找到我家。

朗西洛特：謝謝您，先生！來吧，父親。我馬上去和猶太人道別。

（朗西洛特和他父親下；格拉西安諾上，向巴薩尼歐走來。）

格拉西安諾：巴薩尼歐！

巴薩尼歐：格拉西安諾！

格拉西安諾：我有個請求。

巴薩尼歐：請說。

格拉西安諾：我必須要和你一起去貝爾蒙。

巴薩尼歐：那麼，就這麼決定。但聽著——有時候你太狂野，太無禮，太魯莽。這些特質和你很相稱，對我們來說，似乎也不是缺點。但在陌生人面前，就太放肆了。請努力節制你的行為舉止。你高亢的情緒，可能會害我在貝爾蒙被誤解，並讓我的希望破滅。

格拉西安諾：巴薩尼歐，聽我說。如果我的穿著不樸素，說話不尊重，而且不是只偶爾咒罵幾句，像欲取悅自己祖母的男子一般——那麼，永遠不要再相信我！

巴薩尼歐：很好，我們看看你的表現。

格拉西安諾：但今晚還不算！別用我們今晚的作為來評斷我。

巴薩尼歐：不，那樣就太可惜了。我寧願你表現出最搞笑的一面，因為我們的朋友們都想要好好樂一下。不過，現在先再見了。我還有事要辦。

格拉西安諾：而我現在要去找羅倫佐。我們晚餐時見。

（他們分道揚鑣。）

●第三場 ———————————————————— P. 039

（夏洛克家前門；潔西卡和朗西洛特從屋內出來。）

潔西卡：很遺憾你要離開我父親。不過，再會吧——這個金幣給你。還有，朗西洛特，請私下把這封信交給羅倫佐，你新老爺的客人。

朗西洛特：再會。讓我的眼淚為我說話，就算這些可笑的眼淚不夠有男子氣概。再會了，甜美的潔西卡！

潔西卡：再會，好朗西洛特！（朗西洛特下，擦乾眼淚。）唉，我以身為我父親的孩子為恥，真是罪過啊！我是他女兒，但我不像他。喔，羅倫佐，如果你信守你的諾言，這種衝突就要結束了。我會成為基督徒，以及你鍾愛的妻子。

（她走進屋內。）

●第四場

（威尼斯的另一條街道。格拉西安諾、羅倫佐、撒萊利歐和索拉尼歐上，討論著他們時尚化裝舞會的準備工作。）

羅倫佐：那麼，我們會在晚餐時離開，在我的租屋處換好衣服，然後在一個小時內回來。

格拉西安諾：但我們還沒有準備好。

撒萊利歐：我們還沒有僱到拿火把的人。

索拉尼歐：除非都已安排妥當，否則派對會很無聊。我想，我們不應該舉行。

羅倫佐：現在才四點，我們還有兩個小時可以把一切準備妥當。（朗西洛特上。）朗西洛特，朋友，有什麼新鮮事嗎？

朗西洛特（拿出一封信）：打開它，你就會知道了。

格拉西安諾：我看是情書！

朗西洛特：我先告退了，先生。

（他動身離開。）

羅倫佐：你要去哪裡？

朗西洛特：先生，去邀我的舊主人，那位猶太人，去和我的新主人，那位基督徒，今晚共進晚餐。

羅倫佐：等等，拿著這個。（他給他小費。）告訴親愛的潔西卡，我不會讓她失望。私下告訴她。（朗西洛特下。）來吧，各位。為今晚做好準備。

撒萊利歐：好，我會開始準備。

索拉尼歐：我也是。

羅倫佐：大約一小時後，在格拉西安諾家，和我及格拉西安諾碰面。

撒萊利歐：好主意。

（撒萊利歐及索拉尼歐下。）

格拉西安諾：那封信是美麗的潔西卡寫來的吧？

羅倫佐：我最好全都告訴你。她告訴我把她從她父親家帶走的方法，告訴我她會帶什麼黃金和珠寶，還有她會如何打扮成一個年輕侍從。如果她父親能進入天堂，那會是因為他溫柔和善的女兒之故。願不幸永遠不會阻擋她的道路。和我一起走，一邊走一邊看這封信，美麗的潔西卡會是為我舉火把的人！

（他們輕快地走出去。）

●第五場 ———————————————————— P. 042

（夏洛克與朗西洛特上。）

夏洛克：你會明白的！你的眼睛會評斷出老夏洛克和巴薩尼歐的不同。（大叫。）潔西卡！（對朗西洛特：）你不會像你在我這裡時那樣把自己吃撐。（再次大喊。）潔西卡！（對朗西洛特：）或者睡覺打呼，然後把制服穿破。（更大聲喊。）喂，潔西卡呀！

（潔西卡上。）

潔西卡：你叫我？有什麼事？

夏洛克：我受邀出外吃飯，潔西卡。這是我的鑰匙。但我為什麼要去？他們又不是出於愛才邀我，而是要拍我馬屁。不過，我還是會帶著恨去赴約，去吃那揮霍成性的基督徒的餐點。潔西卡，我的女兒，照顧好我的房子。我不想去，有什麼事情覺得不太對勁。

朗西洛特：我懇求您，先生，去吧！我的年輕主人期待有你為伴的不適。

夏洛克：我對他也是。

143

朗西洛特：而且他們還準備了節目。我不會確切説出，您會看到一場化裝舞會。但是（眨眼。）如果您真的看到那些表演，別吃驚。

夏洛克：什麼，會有化裝舞會？聽好，潔西卡，把我的門鎖好。當你聽到鼓聲以及吹笛手發出的邪惡高音，別往外看街道上那些戴著彩繪面具的愚蠢基督徒。給我的屋子戴上耳塞——別讓那些膚淺的愚蠢聲音進入我莊重的家園。我發誓我一點都不想外出晚餐，但我會去。（對朗西洛特：）你先去吧。通報我會去。

朗西洛特：那我先走了，先生。（對潔西卡竊語：）小姐，注意看窗外，因為（吟誦。）某個基督徒會經過，值得猶太小姐看一眼。

（他離開，吹著口哨。）

夏洛克：那個非猶太笨蛋説什麼？

潔西卡：他説：「再會了，小姐。」就這樣。

夏洛克：這個笨蛋人夠好，但食量太大，工作速度像蝸牛一樣慢，而且他白天睡得比野貓還多。我屋裡不要再養懶人，因此，我讓他走——去別人家幫忙揮霍借來的錢。潔西卡，進去。我也許馬上就回來了。照我的話做，進去後把門關上。

（夏洛克離開。）

潔西卡：再會。如果我沒有錯過好運，我會失去父親，而你會失去女兒。

（潔西卡進入屋內。）

（威尼斯街道；格拉西安諾和撒萊利歐上，戴著面具。）

格拉西安諾：羅倫佐就是要我們在這個陽台下等候。

撒萊利歐：他遲到了。

格拉西安諾：好奇怪，他竟然不在這裡。情侶通常都會早到。

撒萊利歐：看！他現在來了。

（羅倫佐上。）

羅倫佐：好朋友，原諒我遲到了。原因是生意，不是我。來吧。這是我的猶太岳父住的地方。（他出聲喊。）哈囉！有人在家嗎？（一扇窗戶打開，潔西卡現身，打扮成男孩。）

潔西卡：是誰？雖然我想我認得你的聲音，請說出你的名字！

羅倫佐：羅倫佐，你的愛人！

潔西卡：當然是羅倫佐，而且肯定是我的愛！來，接住這只箱子。它值得如此麻煩。（她將它往下扔。）我很高興現在已是夜晚。別看我，因為我羞於展示我的服裝。但愛情是盲目的，而情侶看不到他們自己的愚蠢。如果他們可以，邱比特看到我變裝成男孩，都要臉紅了。

羅倫佐：下來吧，你一定是幫我舉火把的人。

潔西卡：我一定得這麼丟臉地舉著蠟燭嗎？它本身確實已夠亮了。愛情在謙遜中茁壯，而我應該要隱藏起來。

羅倫佐：你是啊，親愛的，就算穿著這身偽裝的可愛男裝也是如此。不過，馬上下來吧。時間愈來愈晚，我們預計要去巴薩尼歐的派對。（她關上窗戶。）（對格拉西安諾：）老天在上，我好愛她！如果我是個法官，她很有智慧，如果我的雙眼沒看錯，她真美！而且她很忠貞，她剛剛也證明如此。因而，她的形象──智慧、美麗而忠貞，永遠停駐於我的靈魂裡。（潔西卡從屋內走出來。）你來了。走吧，各位！我們的朋友正在派對上等我們呢。（他們前往派對。）

（波西亞在貝爾蒙住家的大廳；波西亞上，摩洛哥親王及他們的僕人
和隨從也一併上場。）

波西亞（對僕人）：去，拉開簾子。給尊貴的親王看那三只箱
子。（簾子拉開，露出三只陳列在桌上的箱子。）（對親王：）現
在，請作出你的選擇。

摩洛哥：第一只是金子的，上面有這樣的字句：「選了我的
人，將得到許多男人渴望的東西。」第二只是銀子的，
上面有這樣的承諾：「選了我的人，將得到他所應得的東
西。」第三只，是晦暗無光的鉛，直率地警告：「選了我的
人，必須給予並賭上他的所有一切。」我該怎麼得知我的
選擇是正確的？

波西亞：其中一只裡有我的畫像，親王。如果你選到那一只，
你就會成為我的丈夫。

摩洛哥：祈求神明引導我！讓我看看。這只鉛箱說什麼？
「……必須給予並賭上他的所有一切。」必須給予？為了
什麼？為了鉛？賭上一切為了鉛？這只箱子看起來會帶來
危險。我不會為了鉛而給予或賭上一切。這只銀箱呢？
「……將得到他應得的東西。」暫停一下，摩洛哥。掂掂
你的價值。我應得到足夠的東西，但「足夠」也許不會包
含小姐。然而，我不應該低估自己。得到如同我應得的那
麼多——啊，那就是小姐了！如果我不再繼續，就選這只
呢？讓我們再看一次金箱上說的話。「……將得到許多男
人渴望的東西。」那正是小姐——全世界都渴望她。這三
只箱子有一只裡面有她美若天仙的畫像。她有可能在鉛箱
裡嗎？我想不會。我想她也不會在銀箱裡，那價值比不上
金子。給我鑰匙。我選金箱，我要賭賭運氣！

波西亞（把鑰匙遞給他）：拿去，親王。如果我的畫像在裡面，那麼我就是你的了。

（他打開金箱子。）

摩洛哥：喔，不！這裡面是什麼？一顆腐朽的骷髏頭，空洞的眼窩裡塞著一捲手稿。我來唸出來。「閃亮之物非皆黃金，此番箴言人人常聽。眾人紛紛把命賣，為我容貌一眼看。黃金陵墓藏蛀蟲，你若聰明膽識同，四肢強健智慧久，答案不在紙上留——再會了，你的追求已然終了，無疾而終，功虧一簣。那麼，告別熱情，迎來失敗的冰霜。」波西亞，再會。我的心太悲傷，無法好好道別。因此，失敗者就此離去。

（鞠躬，他和隨從離去。）

波西亞（對奈莉莎）：擺脫得好！（對僕人：）拉上簾子。去。願一切隨他的浮誇離我而去。

（眾人下。）

●第八場 ——————————————P. 052

（威尼斯的街道；撒萊利歐和索拉尼歐上。）

撒萊利歐：怎麼，老兄，我看到巴薩尼歐啟航。格拉西安諾和他一起出發。我確信羅倫佐不在船上。

索拉尼歐：那個可鄙猶太人的吶喊吵醒了公爵，和他一起去搜尋巴薩尼歐的船。

撒萊利歐：他晚了一步，船已經離開。但有人說，看見羅倫佐和潔西卡一起在一艘平底小船上。而且，安東尼歐告訴公爵，他們沒有和巴薩尼歐一起在他的船上。

索拉尼歐：我從來沒聽過像那猶太人在街上發出的那種呼喊。「我的女兒！我的金幣！我的女兒！和一個基督徒跑了！正義！法律！我的金幣，我的女兒！一只密封的袋子！我的女兒從我身邊偷走了兩袋金幣！還有珠寶——兩顆珍貴的寶石——被我的女兒偷走了！找到那女孩！她拿走了寶石和金錢！」

撒萊利歐（大笑）：所有威尼斯的男孩都跟著他，大叫：「他的寶石！他的女兒！他的錢！」

索拉尼歐（現在嚴肅起來）：安東尼歐最好準時付清他的貸款，否則他得為此付出代價。

撒萊利歐：你說得對。我昨天和一個法國人聊天，他說有一艘滿載貨物的威尼斯商船在英吉利海峽沉沒了。他告訴我的時候，我想到了安東尼歐，暗暗希望不是他的船。

索拉尼歐：你最好告訴安東尼歐這件事。但要婉轉地說，這可能會讓他很傷心。

撒萊利歐：地球上找不到更善良的人了！我看到巴薩尼歐和安東尼歐道別。巴薩尼歐說他很快就會回來，安東尼歐說：「別因為我的緣故而倉促行事，你需要留多久就留多久。至於猶太人的合約，別讓它影響了你的愛情大計。要快樂，專注去求愛，還有在當地看來合宜的示愛方法。」這個時候，他的眼裡充滿了淚水。他轉過頭，把手伸到後面，滿懷感情地和巴薩尼歐握手。然後，兩人就此別過。

索拉尼歐：我想，他對他來說就是一切。讓我們去找他，讓他振作高興起來吧。

撒萊利歐：我們就這麼做吧。

（他們下。）

（波西亞在貝爾蒙的住家；箱廳；奈莉莎和一名僕人上。）

奈莉莎：快點！請拉上簾子！亞拉岡親王已發過誓言，現在要過來做選擇了。

（僕人拉上簾子；波西亞、亞拉岡親王，和他們的隨從上。）

波西亞：箱子在那裡，尊貴的親王。如果你選到有我的畫像在內的箱子，我們就立刻成婚。但如果你失敗，你必須立刻離開。

亞拉岡：我知道風險。現在，願幸運之神應許我心裡的希望！金、銀和卑賤的鉛。「選了我的人，必須給予並賭上他所有一切。」（對著鉛箱說話：）你得看起來更動人些，我才會給予並賭上我的所有。金箱寫了什麼？「選了我的人，將得到許多男人渴望的東西。」我不會選許多男人渴望的東西，因為我不像一般大眾。那麼，你，白銀寶盒！再告訴我一次你的話。「選了我的人，將得到他所應得的東西。」那就是我的選擇。給我這只箱子的鑰匙。（他打開銀箱。）裡面是什麼？一幅愚人的畫像，給我一張紙條。我來唸。（看著畫像。）你和波西亞真不像！我的渴望與應得之物也不相稱！我難道只配得到一張小丑的臉嗎？（打開文件唸：）「有人親吻幻影，其福氣也如幻影。有些活著的愚人，我說，他們就像這樣鍍了銀。重要的不是你娶哪個女人，而是我永遠會是你的頭腦。所以，走吧，因為你的時機已飛逝。」（對波西亞：）我在這裡逗留得愈久，看起來就愈愚蠢。帶著一個愚人的腦袋，我前來求婚，但卻帶著兩個離去。親愛的，再會，我會遵守我的承諾，承受我心深處的悲傷。

（他和他的隨從下。）

波西亞（鬆口氣）：另一隻飛身撲向燭火的飛蛾！喔，這些浮誇的傻瓜！以為他們可以作出聰明的選擇。當他們失敗時，他們好吃驚。

奈莉莎：有句老話說得直接——要上吊還是成婚都是運氣。

波西亞：來吧，拉上簾子，奈莉莎。

（她拉上；一名僕人上。）

僕人：小姐，來了位年輕的威尼斯人，他帶來了極貴重的禮物。到目前為止，我還沒見過這麼有希望的愛情專使。

波西亞：來吧，奈莉莎，我很想見見這位似乎有紳士風範的邱比特使者。

奈莉莎：上帝願意的話，但願是巴薩尼歐！

（眾人下。）

第三幕

● 第一場 ——————————————————— P. 059

（夏洛克在威尼斯住家前的街道；索拉尼歐遇到剛從商業中心里亞爾
托過來的撒萊利歐。）

索拉尼歐：里亞爾托有什麼消息？

撒萊利歐：有個故事在傳，説有艘安東尼歐的船，在英吉利
海峽發生船難。

索拉尼歐：那是怎麼回事？他損失了一艘船？

撒萊利歐：我希望他的損失就此打住。

索拉尼歐：讓我立刻説聲「阿門」，以防魔鬼阻撓我禱告，
因為魔鬼以猶太人形象出現了。（夏洛克從他家裡出來。）你
好，夏洛克！有什麼新消息嗎？

夏洛克（憤怒地）：你們知道的——沒有人像你們這般瞭如指
掌——我女兒跑了。

撒萊利歐：當然！我還知道幫她做翅膀的裁縫是誰！

索拉尼歐：夏洛克知道小鳥已準備好飛翔，而且幼鳥離開牠
們的母鳥是很自然的事。

夏洛克：這件事會毀了她！

撒萊利歐：喔，是的，如果魔鬼是她的法官的話。

夏洛克：我自己的骨肉竟造反！

索拉尼歐（假裝誤解）：真想不到，老皮老骨。什麼，以你這把
年紀？

夏洛克：我是指我女兒，是我的骨肉。

撒萊利歐：你的肉和她的肉，差異比烏黑和象牙白還大；你
們的血，差異比紅酒和白酒還多。但是，現在告訴我們，
你可曾聽説安東尼歐在海上是否有所損失？

151

夏洛克：那是我的另一次失敗交易。一個破產的人，一個浪蕩子。他幾乎沒膽在商業中心露臉了。以前總是洋洋得意到鎮上來的人，現在成了乞丐。他最好履行自己的債務！

撒萊利歐：嗯，我相信如果他不能，你也不會要他的肉。說到底，那有什麼用處呢？

夏洛克：拿來當魚餌！如果它餵不了別的東西，可以餵我的復仇心。他羞辱我，阻礙我，取笑我的損失，嘲諷我的獲利。他藐視我的民族，阻撓我的交易，潑我朋友冷水，激怒我的敵人。為什麼呢？我是個猶太人。但猶太人沒有眼睛嗎？猶太人沒有手、器官、四肢、感官、情感、熱情嗎？猶太人不是吃同樣的食物，被同樣的武器所傷，會感染同樣的疾病，用同樣的方法治好，因同樣的冬天和夏天而感覺溫暖和寒冷，一切就像基督徒一樣嗎？如果你們刺我們，我們不會流血嗎？如果你們搔我們癢，我們不會大笑嗎？如果你們給我們下毒，我們不會死掉嗎？而如果你們冤枉我們，我們不會想報仇嗎？如果我們在其他每一方面都像你們，我們在那一方面就也就像你們一樣。如果一個猶太人冤枉了一個基督徒，他的自然反應是什麼？復仇。如果一個基督徒冤枉了一個猶太人，他的懲罰應該是什麼，以基督徒的標準？也是復仇啊！你們教會我的惡行，我會實踐。如果我有機會，我會做得更狠！

（一名僕人攔下索拉尼歐和撒萊利歐。）

僕人：先生，我的主人安東尼歐在家。他有話想和你們兩位說。

撒萊利歐：我們一直在找他。

（索拉尼歐、撒萊利歐和僕人下；杜巴向夏洛克家走來。）

夏洛克：你好，杜巴。熱那亞有什麼消息？你找到我女兒了嗎？

杜巴：我曾聽到她的消息，但我找不到她。

夏洛克：沒有他們的消息？好吧。而且，我也不知道到目前為止的搜尋花了多少錢。損失再加損失！小偷偷走了這麼多，然後花了更多錢去找這個小偷，卻仍無法滿意！無法報仇！別人都沒有惡運，只有惡運掉到我頭上。獨留我一人嘆息，獨自拭淚！

（他哭。）

杜巴：是的，其他人運氣也不好，安東尼歐，如我在熱那亞聽說的……

夏洛克（迅速恢復）：什麼，什麼事？運氣不好？你剛說他運氣不好？

杜巴：他失去了一艘從的黎波里開來的船。

夏洛克：感謝老天爺！是真的嗎？

杜巴：我和幾位從那場船難中逃生的水手談過。

夏洛克：謝謝你，杜巴。好消息！哈，哈！這是你在熱那亞聽到的嗎？

杜巴（改變話題）：我也聽說你女兒一晚上就花掉八十個金幣。

夏洛克：你刺了我一刀！我再也看不到我的金子了。一口氣八十個金幣！八十個金幣！

杜巴（又換回原來話題）：好幾位安東尼歐的債權人來威尼斯找我。他們信誓旦旦地說，他就快破產了。

夏洛克：我真高興聽到這件事。我要糾纏他，我要折磨他。聽聞此事真令我開心！

杜巴（又跳回去談潔西卡）：其中一人給我看一枚戒指，你女兒拿這個來和他換了一隻猴子。

夏洛克：你在折磨我，杜巴！那只戒指是莉亞在我們結婚前給我的，我可不會拿來換一隻野猴子。

杜巴（試著安撫夏洛克的痛苦）：但安東尼歐肯定完蛋了。

夏洛克：對，沒錯。去，找個警長來。我要給安東尼歐兩個星期的時間，如果他還不出錢，我就要他的心！等他被趕出威尼斯，我就可以照我的方式做生意了。去吧，杜巴，到我們的猶太教堂和我碰面。

（他們下，分道揚鑣。）

●第二場 ─────────────────── P. 065

（波西亞在貝爾蒙住家的大廳；簾子已拉開，露出箱子；巴薩尼歐準備做選擇。）

波西亞：請等一下。在你冒險之前，先等一或二天。如果你選錯，我就沒有你作伴了。因此，等一段時間吧。我的感覺告訴我，我不想失去你。你自己知道，恨是不會給出這種建議的。但避免你並未清楚認識我這個人──因為未婚少女的想法只能放在心裡，不能講出來──我想把你先留在這裡一或二個月，你再做出選擇。我可以教你如何正確選擇，但我發過誓不能這麼做。如果你沒有贏，我也永遠不會屬於別人。如果你失敗了，你會讓我萌生不道德的念頭──要是我打破誓言並給你建議就好了。你的眼睛真可惡！它們看著我，把我分成了兩半。一半的我是你的，另一半，也是。我應該說「我自己的」，但我的就是你的，因此，全部的我都是你的。我話太多了，但這是為了讓時間慢下來，把它拉長，延伸以拖延你做出選擇。

巴薩尼歐：讓我選吧。我現在這樣，是活在極端的痛苦裡。

波西亞：十分痛苦，巴薩尼歐！那麼，坦白說出，你的愛混合了何種的背叛！

巴薩尼歐：只有醜惡的不信任，讓我害怕，不敢享受我的愛情。雪與火倒不如成為朋友，猶如背叛與我的愛情。

波西亞：是的，但我擔心痛苦會讓你口不擇言，就像任何受到痛苦折磨的人一樣。

巴薩尼歐：饒恕我的生命，我就供出真相！

波西亞：那麼，坦承一切並活下去吧。

巴薩尼歐：「坦承一切並去愛」，是我的全部供詞。喔，快樂的折磨，折磨我的人給了我讓我獲釋的答案。但讓我試試我在箱子上的運氣吧。

波西亞：那麼，去吧！我被鎖在其中一只裡面。如果你真的愛我，你就會找到我。（*對旁觀者：*）奈莉莎和其他人，站到旁邊去。讓音樂在他選擇時演奏。那樣的話，如果他選錯了，他就可以像垂死的天鵝般離去，漸漸消失在音樂中。（*一個僕人留下，其他人往音樂廳而去。*）為了延伸這個比喻，我的淚水將是溪河，是他的死之水床。（*情緒高昂些。*）他可能會贏，那麼音樂又當何用？喔，那麼，音樂就像黎明的合唱團，爬進睡夢中的新郎耳中，喚醒他前往他的婚禮。他走過去了。（*對巴薩尼歐：*）去吧，愛人！如果你贏了，我就活了！

（*音樂響起，巴薩尼歐在思索。*）

巴薩尼歐：世界被外表的裝飾所蒙蔽。在法庭上，不管多腐敗的辯詞都可以把它的邪惡藏在神聖的話語中。在宗教上，只要有學問的人引用《聖經》來支持任何異端邪說的粗俗，就可以讓這些言論得到祝福。有多少懦夫，心像用沙搭建的樓梯一樣虛假，卻像勇敢的大力士海克力斯和好鬥的戰神一樣留著鬍子？他們留著那樣的鬍子，只是要看起來很強悍。看看美貌。你會看到它通常以盎司來論買賣。化妝品效果神奇，那些道德最薄弱的人，用得最凶。裝飾品就像是有著最凶險海洋的岩岸，是掩飾未知美貌的美麗圍巾。因此，華麗而俗氣的黃金，我一點也不想要你。也不要你，白銀，用以製造一般錢幣的物質。但是你，沒有價值的鉛，寧願威脅也不願許下承諾，你的黯淡比華麗詞藻更感動我。我選你，願喜樂是結果！

（僕人遞給他鑰匙。）

波西亞（竊語）：其他的激情多快消失啊——懷疑、絕望、恐懼和嫉妒！喔，愛情，要謙卑，控制你的狂喜，克制你的歡樂！別太激動，我感受到你太多的祝福了，讓它少一點，以免它把我淹沒了！

巴薩尼歐（打開箱子）：這是什麼？美麗波西亞的畫像！（讚嘆畫像。）女神！這雙眼會動嗎？或者，它們只是反映了我的動作？這雙唇會吐出甜美的氣息！這畫家像蜘蛛一樣，在她的髮絲中織了一張金網，比捕捉蛛網上的小蟲還快速地捕獲男人的心。但她的眼睛！他怎麼能睜著眼畫完呢？在他畫完一隻後，它的力量應該就讓他失明，使他無法畫出相匹配的另一隻眼。但看啊！就像我的讚美拉低了這幅畫的價值，這幅畫也遠遠不及真人。這裡是這卷軸，我的命運就總結於此：（他唸卷軸。）「你不依外表而選擇，願意孤注一擲只求公正，因此選擇結果如你所望。既然這般好運降臨你身，記得滿足莫再尋求新人。若你對此般結果心滿意足，認為此等好運就是大福，就快轉向佳人，深情一吻。」真是體貼的卷軸！（他轉向波西亞。）我來向你請求許可，徵詢你的同意。（呈上卷軸，當作請求一吻的許可。）給出並接受一個吻，但只有你願意才行，我等著聽到你的真心回應。

波西亞：你看我，巴薩尼歐大人，真實的我。為我自己，我不會想要改善。但為了你，我希望我能更好六十倍，更美千倍，更富萬倍。我真的很微不足道——頂多是位沒受過教育，沒見過世面的女孩。還好，沒有老到學不動，更好的是，沒有笨到學不會，最好的是，我將自己獻給你，我的主人、總督和國王。（他們接吻，達成卷軸的條件。）我自己，以及我的財產，現在是你的了。直到這一刻，我都是這間豪宅的領主，我僕人的主人，我自己的女王。現在，這間房子、這些僕人和我自己，都是你的。我以這枚戒指將他們給你。（她把一只戒指套到巴薩尼歐的手指上。）如果你和這只戒指分開、遺失了它，或把它送人，那就代表你的愛情的終結，也是我要譴責你的理由。

巴薩尼歐：小姐，我不知道要說什麼了！只有我血管裡的血在和你說話。我就像群眾一樣，因受人愛戴的親王的一番動人演說而歡欣鼓舞。我身體的每個原子都在瘋狂吶喊著欣喜的歡呼。當這只戒指與這隻手指分離時，就是生命離我而去之時。然後你可以肯定地說：「這表示巴薩尼歐已死。」

（奈莉莎與格拉西安諾加入他們。）

奈莉莎：真高興啊，大人和小姐！

格拉西安諾：巴薩尼歐大人和溫柔的小姐，我祝你們滿懷欣喜。當你們結婚的時刻來臨，我懇求你，那時也能讓我成婚！

巴薩尼歐：當然，如果你能找到一位妻子。

格拉西安諾：謝謝你，大人，你已幫我找到一個。（他拉起奈莉莎的手。）我的雙眼，大人，就像你的一樣快。你看到了女主人，而我看到了侍女。你戀愛了，我也戀愛了。你的命運取決於那邊的箱子，我的也是，而結果也夢想成真。我求婚直到我汗濕，說愛的誓言直說到我嘴乾。最後，我從這位美麗的小姐這裡，得到她的許諾，條件是你能贏得她家女主人的芳心。

波西亞：這是真的嗎，奈莉莎？

奈莉莎：小姐，是的，如果你滿意。

巴薩尼歐：你是真心的嗎，格拉西安諾？

格拉西安諾：的確是的，大人。

巴薩尼歐：我們的婚宴會因你們的婚禮而得到至上的光榮。

格拉西安諾（對奈莉莎）：我們與他們打賭一千金幣，我們會先生兒子。

奈莉莎（臉紅）：什麼，要賭那個？

格拉西安諾（戲弄）：若不快點行動，我們就贏不了！（羅倫佐和潔西卡上，後面跟著撒萊利歐，拿著一封信。）這是誰來了？羅倫佐和潔西卡？什麼？還有我的威尼斯老友，撒萊利歐？

巴薩尼歐：羅倫佐和撒萊利歐，歡迎。如果一個才剛擁有我在這裡地位的人可以這麼做的話，我歡迎你們。（對波西亞：）希望你能許可，甜美的波西亞。

波西亞：當然歡迎他們，大人。

羅倫佐（對巴薩尼歐）：謝謝你的隆情。就我來說，我原先沒打算來這裡找你。但我在路上遇到撒萊利歐，他求我一起來。他不許我拒絕。

撒萊利歐：是的，大人，我有好理由。（他把信給巴薩尼歐。）安東尼歐請我代為問候。

巴薩尼歐：在我拆開他的信之前，告訴我，我的好友最近好嗎？

撒萊利歐：沒生病——除非是精神上。但也不好，除非你是指精神上。他的信解釋了他的狀況。

（巴薩尼歐拆開信。）

格拉西安諾（朝潔西卡點頭）：奈莉莎，給我們的陌生人打打氣。歡迎她。（奈莉莎問候潔西卡，格拉西安諾和撒萊利歐握手。）給我你的手，撒萊利歐。威尼斯有什麼消息？安東尼歐好嗎？我知道他會為我們高興！

撒萊利歐：他會為你們高興，我確信。但他的生意進展得並不順利。

（他把格拉西安諾拉到一旁解釋。）

波西亞（觀察讀信的巴薩尼歐）：那封信裡有令人傷心的消息，讓巴薩尼歐臉上失去血色。某個親愛的朋友去世了？什麼，更糟？（她碰他的手臂。）懷著敬意，巴薩尼歐，我是你的一半。我很樂意分擔一半這封信帶給你的任何煩惱。

巴薩尼歐：體貼的波西亞！這裡是曾出現在紙上，最令人傷心的話語之一！親愛的小姐，當我一開始向你表達愛意時，我直率地坦承，我所有的財產都在我的血管裡。我是個紳士，因此我告訴你實情。但是，親愛的小姐，當我告訴你，我一無所有，你將會發現我在吹牛。我應該告訴你，我擁有的比一無所有還要少。事實上，我受惠於一位珍貴的朋友，他向他最大的敵人借貸來借給我用。這裡是封信，小姐，這紙張代表我朋友的身體，上面的每一個字都是個裂開的傷口，流出他的生命之血來。但這是真的嗎，撒萊利歐，他所有的投資都付諸流水了嗎？沒有一艘逃過一劫？從的黎波里、墨西哥、英格蘭？從里斯本、巴巴利、印度？沒有一艘船逃過海難之岩的可怕一觸嗎？

159

撒萊利歐：無一倖免，大人。此外，看起來就算他能還清借款，猶太人也不願拿錢。我從來不知道有這麼個人形怪物，這麼強烈而飢渴地要毀掉一個人。他每天早晚向公爵訴求，說不給他公平正義是不合法的。公爵、貴族和二十名商人和他辯論。但他不聽。

潔西卡：當我和他住在一起時，我聽到他詛咒，寧願得到安東尼歐的肉，也不要二十倍他所欠款項的金額。我知道，大人，如果法律、當局和政府不阻止他的話，可憐的安東尼歐就有苦頭吃了。

波西亞：安東尼歐就是你可貴的朋友嗎？

巴薩尼歐：我最珍貴的朋友。最仁慈的人，最有善意，也是行善者中最孜孜不倦的一位。他身上所具備的羅馬情操比任何一位義大利人還多。

波西亞：他欠猶太人多少錢？

巴薩尼歐：因為我的緣故，三千金幣。

波西亞：就這樣？還他六千！不，再加倍，然後三倍！沒有一個被如此形容的朋友，要因為巴薩尼歐的過失而損失一根頭髮。先跟我到教堂去，娶我為妻，然後去威尼斯找你的朋友，你不能心神不寧地躺在波西亞身旁。帶著足夠的黃金，去付清那小小債務的二十倍有餘。還清後，把你那位真朋友帶來這裡。在你回來之前，奈莉莎和我會以侍女和寡婦的身分生活。現在，去吧！你必須在你的大喜之日離開。歡迎你的朋友。微笑！因為你是高價得來，我會深情愛你。讓我聽聽你朋友的信。

巴薩尼歐（讀信）：「親愛的巴薩尼歐，我的船隻全數沉沒。我的債權人益發殘酷，而我的資產極為稀少。我和猶太人簽的借據要開罰。還完債後，我不可能活下來。但我們之間的債務將一筆勾銷——如果，在我死時，我能見你一面。
儘管如此，照你的意思做。如果你對我的愛，不足以說服
你前來，別讓這封信說服你來。」

波西亞：喔，我的愛人！快去救他！

巴薩尼歐：既然你已答應，我就走。但是，在我回來前，我將
不睡也不休息！

（眾人急忙離開。）

● 第三場 P. 078

（夏洛克家外；夏洛克站在門口，和安東尼歐、索拉尼歐及獄卒一起。）

夏洛克：獄卒，看好他！別跟我談慈悲！這就是那個借錢給人
不收利息的傻瓜。獄卒，看好他。

安東尼歐：聽我說一下，好夏洛克——

夏洛克：我要履行我的借據！別出言否定我的借據。我已發
過誓，我會履行我的借據。你毫無理由就罵我是狗，既
然我是狗，小心我的尖牙！公爵會答應給我正義。我很吃
驚，你這個缺德的獄卒，竟然這麼蠢，在他的請求下，帶
著他到處走！

安東尼歐：拜託，聽我說！

夏洛克：我要照借據走。別說話！我不會再被搞成一個心軟
又愚蠢的傻瓜，搖頭、嘆氣，然後屈服於基督徒的請求。
別跟著我。別和我說話！我要照借據走！

（他進入屋內，甩上門。）

索拉尼歐：他真是與人為伴的所有狗裡最頑固的一隻。

安東尼歐：別管他了。我不會再拿無用的請求，追著他跑了。他要我的命，我很清楚他的理由。我常在別人請我幫忙時，替別人償還債務給他。所以，他恨我。

索拉尼歐：我確定，公爵絕不會作出有利這借據條款的判決。

安東尼歐：公爵無法更改法律。如果我們否認威尼斯此地外國人的權利，它會抵觸我們的公義概念。這城市和世界各國的人貿易。我因為悲傷與損失，已經瘦了好多磅，明天我幾乎擠不出一磅肉給我那嗜血的債主了。獄卒，我們走吧。但願巴薩尼歐能來，看我付清他的債務。那我就心滿意足了！

（眾人下。）

●第四場 —————————————————— P. 081

（波西亞在貝爾蒙的住家；波西亞、奈莉莎、羅倫佐、潔西卡及波西亞的僕人巴爾薩澤上。）

羅倫佐：小姐，你對友誼有真誠而高貴的了解。如果你認識你所尊敬的男人——他是多麼標準的一位紳士，他與你夫君的感情多麼深厚——我知道你對你的作為會更加自豪。

波西亞：我從來不懊悔做善事，現在也不會。這兩位朋友經常一起交談並消磨時間，而且兩人同樣愛著彼此，他們一定在精神上有類似之處。這讓我思索，安東尼歐身為我夫君的好朋友，一定和他很像。如果是這樣，我將一位靈魂伴侶從地獄般的酷刑中解救出來，代價是多麼低廉啊。這聽起來很像在讚美我自己，所以，說夠多了！換個話題，羅倫佐，我要你在我夫君回來之前，接管我宅子的管理工作。至於我自己，我已悄悄立誓，除了奈莉莎作伴外，我要獨自禱告與冥想，直到我們的夫君回來。兩哩之外有家修道院，我們會住在那裡。我希望你不要拒絕我的請求，我是出於愛與迫切的需要才提出的。

羅倫佐：小姐，我會全心全意遵守你的指示。

波西亞：我的僕人都已知道我的計畫。他們會接受你和潔西卡取代巴薩尼歐大人和我的地位。那麼，在相逢前再會了！

羅倫佐：再會了，小姐。

（潔西卡和羅倫佐下。）

波西亞：現在，巴爾薩澤！你一直都很真誠，讓我知道你現在也是。（交給他一封信。）拿著這封信，儘快趕到帕多瓦去。把這封信交給我表哥貝拉利歐博士。他會交給你一些文件和衣服。把它們帶到往威尼斯的公共渡輪渡口。別浪費時間問話，快去吧！我會先去那裡等你。

巴爾薩澤：小姐，我會儘快趕去。

（他下。）

波西亞：來吧，奈莉莎。我有你不知道的工作要做。我們會在我們的夫君想到我們之前，先看到他們。

奈莉莎：他們會看到我們嗎？

波西亞：他們會，奈莉莎，但他們會從我們的衣著認為我們
　　　是男人。我和你打賭，等我們打扮成年輕人，我會是兩人
　　　裡較英俊的那個。我會更英勇地配戴著匕首，用稚嫩年輕
　　　人的高音說話，把我那年輕女子的步伐轉變成男人的大
　　　步走，並像愛吹牛的年輕人一樣，吹噓打架的事。我會撒
　　　謊，說我傷了多少人的心。如此一來，人們會斷言，我離開
　　　學校至少已有一年了。

奈莉莎：什麼，我們要變成男人？

波西亞：天啊！這是什麼好笑的問題！但來吧。等我們坐上馬
　　　車，我會告訴你我的計畫，馬車在花園大門口等著呢。我
　　　們趕快走，今天得趕二十哩路！

（她們匆忙離開。）

第四幕

●第一場

（威尼斯法庭，安東尼歐由兩名獄警帶著，後面跟著巴薩尼歐、格拉西安諾、索拉尼歐、官員和書記員，最後面是公爵。）

公爵：安東尼歐來了嗎？

安東尼歐：在這裡，大人。

公爵：我著實為你難過。你來此要與一個鐵石心腸的敵人對質，他野蠻卑鄙且無憐憫之心，連一絲慈悲都沒有！

安東尼歐：我會以耐心來迎接他的憤怒，我已準備好以平靜的心情忍受他的怒火。

公爵：來人，叫猶太人上庭。

索拉尼歐：他已經在門口了。他來了，大人。

公爵：讓路給他，讓他站到我面前來。（*群眾分開，夏洛克站在公爵面前，深深鞠躬。*）夏洛克，大家都覺得——我也是——你打算懷著這股怨恨直到最後。然後，大家以為你會表現出比如此明顯的殘忍更加奇怪的慈悲與自責。而你現在要求收到罰款，也就是這位可憐商人的一磅肉，你最終會大發慈悲，被人類的溫柔和愛所感動，你甚至會免除部分原來的債務。有人說，你會因為他近日遭逢的重大損失而同情他。那樣的損失會壓垮一位優秀的商人，讓最無情的心受到感動。（*他暫停。*）我們都期待一個和善的回應，夏洛克。

夏洛克：我已向大人稟告過我的想法。我已向我們的勝安息日發過誓，要拿回借據上拖欠的所有金額。如果你不允諾，危險將降臨你城市的憲法與自由。你會問我，為何我選擇要一磅無用的肉，而不要接受三千金幣。我不願意

第四幕 / 第一場 (sidebar)

回答這個問題！就說那是我的突發奇想吧！這樣算回答了嗎？如果我家裡受老鼠所擾，而我很樂意出一萬金幣來毒死牠呢？這是好答案嗎？我不會再給出任何理由，除了我對安東尼歐的深仇大恨，才會和他打一場會輸的官司。你得到你的答案了嗎？

巴薩尼歐：這不是答案，你這冷血無情的人，替你的殘忍找藉口！

夏洛克：我沒有義務要給出讓你滿意的回答！

巴薩尼歐：所有的人都會毀掉他們不愛的東西嗎？

夏洛克：任何人不是都想毀掉他痛恨的東西嗎？

巴薩尼歐：不是每個引人反感的事物都會導致仇恨。

夏洛克：怎麼，你會讓一條蛇咬你兩次嗎？

安東尼歐（對巴薩尼歐）：你以為你可以和猶太人講道理嗎？你還不如去站在海灘，告訴海浪不要打到它平常的高度。或者，你不如去問野狼，牠為什麼要害母羊為小羊哭泣。你不如禁止山上的松樹在被強風吹襲時，不可以搖擺或發出聲音。那麼困難的事，你不如都嘗試去做，一如嘗試軟化最堅硬的東西——他的心。因此，我懇求你不要再提出建議，不要再想法子。請儘快讓我知道法庭的判決，並讓猶太人得償所願！

巴薩尼歐：我願給你那三千金幣的兩倍！

夏洛克：就算你將每個六千金幣都分成六份，每一份是一個金幣，我也不會要。我要求履行借據！

公爵：當你一點慈悲也不願意給時，又如何能希望人家以悲憫之心待你？

夏洛克：若我行事無錯，我又為何要害怕判決？你們很多人都有奴隸，你們把他們當作你們的狗和騾——做著痛苦的工作，因為你花錢買了他們。我該對你們説：「放他們自由，讓他們和你們的繼承人結婚。他們為什麼要負著重擔而流汗？讓他們的床像你們的一樣柔軟，食物也同你們的一樣好吧。」你們會回答：「奴隸是屬於我們的。」而我也會説一樣的話。我要求他的那一磅肉，是高價買來的。那是我的，我要它。如果你們否決，我鄙視你們的法律！威尼斯的法令沒有效力。我堅持要公理。回答我！我會得到嗎？

公爵：我有權解散這次審判，除非貝拉利歐今天能來此地，他是一位博學的法律博士，我為了解決這個案子已派人去請他。

索拉尼歐：大人，一位使者剛從帕多瓦抵達，帶著博士的信函。

公爵：把信拿來給我。

巴薩尼歐：高興點，安東尼歐！要勇敢！在你為了我而失去一滴血之前，猶太人可以先拿走我的肉、血、骨，以及一切。

（夏洛克拿出一把刀，開始在他皮鞋的鞋底上磨利刀子。）

安東尼歐：我是羊群裡最虛弱的公羊，最適合被宰殺。發育最不良的果子會最先掉落，因此就讓我落下吧。你的最大用途，巴薩尼歐，就是活著幫我寫墓誌銘。

（奈莉莎上，穿著法官書記員的服裝。）

公爵：你是貝拉利歐派來的嗎？

奈莉莎：是的，他致上問候。

（她呈上一封信，公爵讀著。）

巴薩尼歐（對夏洛克）：你為什麼這麼急著磨刀子呢？

夏洛克：為了割取我那一磅肉。

格拉西安諾：你不是在鞋底磨刀，而是在你永生的靈魂上！沒有金屬，甚至是劊子手的斧頭，有你那強烈嫉妒心的一半尖利！沒有任何祈求能感動你嗎？

夏洛克：從你腦子想出來的都沒用。

格拉西安諾：該死的，你這隻頑固的老狗！司法要因為讓你活著而受譴責。我幾乎要懷疑我的信仰，並相信動物的靈魂能進入人體的説法了。你的靈魂來自野狼，牠因為咬死人而被吊死，那時牠的靈魂飛入你不聖潔的母親的子宮裡，並且進入你的體內！你的慾望像狼一般凶殘、嗜血、卑鄙、飢渴！

夏洛克：除非你能把我借據上的印信移除，否則你説得那麼用力，只是傷害你的肺而已。我是為了司法公義而來。

公爵：這封貝拉利歐的信推薦一位年輕又博學的法學博士來我們的庭上。他在哪裡？

奈莉莎：他就在附近等候您的回覆，您要讓他進來嗎？

公爵：誠摯地邀請他。你們三或四個人，去護送他進來。（隨從下。）現在，庭上的人聽聽貝拉利歐的來信。（他讀信。）「大人，接獲您的來信，我正生著重病。但當您的使者前來時，一位來自羅馬的年輕法學博士正來此拜訪我。我告訴他夏洛克與安東尼歐的官司，我們一起查詢了許多書籍。我請他代替我去見您。我請求您，不要因為他年輕就低估他的能力。我從來不知道，這麼年輕的人，能有這麼老成的頭腦。我相信您會認可他，他的表現自能説明一切。」（他抬頭。）你們都聽到貝拉利歐來信的內容了。（波西亞上，打扮成法官，拿著一本法典。）我想，現在來的是博士本人吧。（他迎接她。）把手伸出來。（他們握手。）你是從老貝拉利歐那裡來的？

波西亞：是的，大人。

公爵：歡迎你。請坐。（一名法警引導波西亞到一張靠近公爵的桌子。）你在來法庭前已熟悉這個案子了嗎？

波西亞：是的，我知道。哪一位是商人，哪一位是猶太人？

公爵：安東尼歐與夏洛克，請起立。

波西亞：你的名字是夏洛克？

夏洛克：夏洛克是我的名字。

波西亞：你的案子很不尋常。但案子很合法，威尼斯的法律無法阻止你打官司。（對安東尼歐：）你遭受到來自他的威脅，不是嗎？

安東尼歐：是的，他是這麼主張。

波西亞：你承認這張借據嗎？

安東尼歐：是的。

波西亞：那麼，猶太人必得發慈悲心了。

夏洛克：是什麼要迫使我這麼做？告訴我！

波西亞：慈悲的本質不能勉強。它像是來自天上的溫柔雨滴落入下方的土地。它有雙倍的祝福。他祝福施予的人，也祝福接受的人。它在最有勢力的人手裡力量最大，它比皇冠更適合國王。國王的權杖展示他的世俗權力，象徵他的敬畏與威權，也是國王之所以受到畏懼的原因。但慈悲高於這種被授予的統治王權，它在國王的心中佔有最高的地位，它是神本身的一種特質。當慈悲與公義取得平衡時，世俗的權勢會最接近神的力量。因此，猶太人，雖然你要求公平正義，請思考：如果只有公平正義勝出的話，我們沒有人可以期待救贖。我們祈求要有慈悲，而這樣的祈禱也教會我們所有人行慈悲之事。我說這一切是為了緩和你所要求的公平正義，如果你堅持，恪守律法的威尼斯法庭只能宣布對那位商人施予刑罰。

夏洛克：我會承擔我自己的罪惡！我要法律執行我的借據！

波西亞：他無法還錢嗎？

巴薩尼歐：他可以的，我已提出在法庭上拿出錢來還他，是兩倍的金額。如果那不夠，我會付十倍的金額。或者把我的手、我的頭、我的心拿去！如果這還不夠，那麼真相後面就藏著怨毒。（他跪在波西亞面前，彷彿在祈求。）我懇求您：以您之力扭轉法律，做一件大好事，犯點小錯，不要讓這個殘忍的魔鬼如償所願！

波西亞：那是不可能的。威尼斯無人有權能改變既定的法律。那會創下先例，而這個例子會引發許多錯誤。不能這樣做。

夏洛克：喔，明智的年輕法官，我崇敬您！

（他親吻她的長袍摺邊。）

波西亞：請讓我看一下借據。

夏洛克（呈上借據）：在這裡，最可敬的博士，在這裡！

波西亞（接過文件但沒看）：夏洛克，有人要還你三倍債務的金額。

夏洛克：我的誓言！我的誓言！我向上天發過誓！我的靈魂要背負背信之罪嗎？不，就算為了全威尼斯也不行！

波西亞（讀借據）：唉呀，這借據是有罰則的。猶太人可以依此合法地要求一磅肉，由他從最靠近商人心臟之處割下。（對夏洛克：）有點慈悲心，收下三倍的錢。叫我把借據撕毀。

夏洛克：等到依據合約付清以後再撕。你看來是個好法官，你懂得法律。以法律之名，我要求判決。

安東尼歐：我強烈要求庭上作出判決。

波西亞（對安東尼歐）：那麼，判決如下：你必須讓你的胸膛準備好挨他的刀子。

夏洛克：真是位高貴的法官！傑出的年輕人！

波西亞：法律的用途在支撐刑罰的合法性，（指著借據。）根據這借據，看來是該支付的。

夏洛克：說得很對，喔，有智慧的法官！

波西亞（對安東尼歐）：那麼，坦露你的胸膛吧。

夏洛克：沒錯，就是他的胸口。借據上是這麼說的：「最靠近他心臟之處。」就是這幾個字。

波西亞：是這樣沒錯。這裡有秤嗎，用來稱肉？

夏洛克：我已準備好了。

（他拉開他的斗蓬，露出秤來。）

波西亞：找一個醫師待命，夏洛克，以止住他的傷口，他才不會因血流不止而亡。

夏洛克：借據上有這麼說嗎？

（他拿起文件來讀。）

波西亞：並沒有明白記載，但那有什麼關係嗎？你會出於慈悲而做這件事。

夏洛克：我找不到這一條，借據上沒寫。

（他把文件遞回去。）

波西亞：商人，你有什麼話要說。

安東尼歐：沒什麼，我已作好準備。巴薩尼歐，把手給我。再會了，別為此事悲傷。我的情形，命運之神已經比平常仁慈了。通常，她會讓不幸的人財產耗盡而苟活，以凹陷的眼窩，起皺的額頭忍受著老年的貧窮，她已免除我受那種凌遲的悲慘生活。請代我向你高尚的夫人問候，告訴她安東尼歐如何就死，還有我有多愛你。當我死後，請說我的好話。等這事講完，請她判斷，巴薩尼歐是否曾被疼愛。

你只要懊悔失去你的朋友，但他並不後悔為你還債。如果猶太人割得夠深，我就能用我全部的心，立刻還清！

巴薩尼歐：安東尼歐，我娶了一個妻子，我愛她如我愛生命。但對我來説，生命、妻子和全世界，都比不上你的命珍貴。我願失去一切──是的，犧牲他們全部──來救你！

波西亞：你的妻子不會因此感謝你的，如果她聽到你提出這樣的條件。

格拉西安諾：我有一個妻子，我發誓我愛她。我但願她在天堂，這樣她就可以懇求某些神力來改變這個猶太人！

奈莉莎：還好，你是在她背後説這種話。那樣的希望會把家裡弄得不愉快的。

夏洛克（竊語）：這些基督徒丈夫！我有個女兒，我寧願她隨便嫁給任何人，就是不要嫁基督徒！（大聲説。）我們在浪費時間。我請求您，開始行刑。

波西亞：那個商人的一磅肉是你的了。法庭給予你，法律也准許。

夏洛克：你是最正直的法官！

波西亞：你必須從他的胸膛割取。法律許可你，法庭給予你。

夏洛克：最博學的法官！判決行刑了！（他以刀指著安東尼歐，朝他走去。）來吧，準備好！

波西亞：等一下，還有一件事。這張借據沒有給你一滴血。正確的字詞是「一磅肉」，因此，你可以拿走你的債務和你的一磅肉。但是，如果在割肉時，你灑出一滴基督徒的血，你的土地和財產，依照威尼斯的法律，將被威尼斯政府沒收。

夏洛克（驚駭）：法律是這樣規定嗎？

波西亞（打開法典）：你可以自己看看。你迫切要求公平正義，而你必定會得到比你所想還更多的正義。

格拉西安諾：喔，博學的法官！

夏洛克：那麼，我接受出價的金額，付我欠款金額的三倍，然後放他走。

巴薩尼歐：錢在這裡。

波西亞（舉起手）：且慢！猶太人將得到公平正義。他除了一磅肉，什麼也得不到。

格拉西安諾：喔，正直、博學的法官！

波西亞：因此，準備割肉吧，不能灑出血來，而且要割下不多也不少的一磅肉。如果你割下多於或少於一磅的肉，即使差別是一盎司的二十分之一──如果秤子會因一根頭髮那樣的重量而些微偏移──那麼，你就得死，而且你所有的財產都會被充公。你為什麼停下來？拿取你的一磅肉吧。

夏洛克（受挫）：把我的錢給我，然後讓我走。

巴薩尼歐：我已準備好要給你了，錢在這裡。

波西亞：他在法庭上公開拒絕了，他將得到完全的公平正義與借據的履行。

夏洛克：連拿回我的錢都不行？

波西亞：除了一磅肉，你什麼也拿不到。而那要冒險取得，猶太人。

夏洛克：我不要再忍受這把戲了！

（他轉身離開。）

波西亞：等一下，猶太人。法律對你還有另一項規定。（她再度查閱法典。）這是威尼斯的一條法令，如果查證屬實，一個外國人直接或間接意圖謀取任何市民的性命，他意圖傷害的人可以拿取他一半的財產。另一半收歸公庫。違法者的命全憑公爵大發慈悲。（她闔上法典。）從你的行為顯示出，你同時間接和直接地密謀殺害被告本人，你的確有被判死刑之虞。因此，跪下來，懇求公爵慈悲。

公爵：為了展示我們靈魂的不同，在你開口懇求之前，我就先饒你一命。你一半的財產歸安東尼歐所有，另一半歸國庫。你悔罪的話，可以將這刑罰改為罰金。

波西亞：是的，國庫的那一半，不是安東尼歐那一半。

夏洛克：不，把我的命一起拿去吧！別饒我一命。你拿走我的收入來源，就是拿走了我的房屋。你拿走我賴以為生的生計，即是拿走了我的生命。

波西亞：你要如何寬待他，安東尼歐？

安東尼歐：如果法庭願意放棄國庫那一半，我會很高興，而讓另一半在他有生之年為我所用。在他死後，我會將它交給近日和他女兒私奔的那位先生。還有另外兩個條件。第一：為了交換這個恩惠，他要立刻成為基督徒。第二：他要在法庭上立下遺囑，死後將所有財產都留給他的女婿羅倫佐和他女兒。

公爵：很好。他得這麼做，否則我就收回我剛剛對他頒布的赦免令！

波西亞：你同意嗎，猶太人？

夏洛克：我同意。

波西亞（對奈莉莎）：書記，草擬一份遺囑。

夏洛克：請允許我離開。我人不舒服。之後再把遺囑送來，我會簽署的。

公爵：你可以離開了，但務必要簽字！（夏洛克下，成了個破產的人。）安東尼歐，報答這位年輕人。我想，你欠他很多。

（公爵與他的隨從下。）

巴薩尼歐（對波西亞）：我的好先生，我的朋友和我因為您的智慧，而免除了極刑。我們很樂意將要支付給猶太人的三千金幣，致贈給您。

安東尼歐：並且，懷著愛與感激，我們欠您的遠大於此數，一輩子都是。

波西亞（婉拒金錢）：心滿意足即是最大的報酬。而救了你，我很滿足。因此，我認為自己已得到很好的報酬。（鞠躬。）祈禱吧，希望我們再相遇時，你們還能記得我。

（她準備離開。）

巴薩尼歐（攔下她）：親愛的先生，我必須再次請求您，收下我們的禮物，這是一分心意，不是費用。我求您兩件事，原諒我的堅持，還有，不要拒絕。

波西亞：你這麼極力勸說，我只好欣然接受。把你的手套給我，我會為你之故而戴著它們。（巴薩尼歐脫下手套。）另外，為了紀念你的厚愛，我要拿走你的這只戒指。（巴薩尼歐突然縮手。）別把手縮回去。你當然不會拒絕給我這個吧？

巴薩尼歐：但這只戒指，好先生——唉呀，這只是個小玩意，我怎麼好意思送你這個。

波西亞：我只想要這只戒指，別的都不要。我已經迷上它了。

巴薩尼歐：這只戒指對我的重要性，遠高於它的價值。我願給你威尼斯最貴重的戒指。我會公告周知，把它找來給你。無意冒犯，但請你務必原諒我這麼做。

波西亞：我明白了，先生，你的提議很大方。首先你教我如何懇求，然後，現在你又教我該如何回應一個乞丐。

巴薩尼歐：好先生，這只戒指是我的妻子送我的。當她把它戴在我手上時，她讓我發誓，要我絕不把它賣掉，也不會送給別人，或將它遺失。

波西亞：那是很多男人不願送禮時用的藉口。如果你的妻子知道我有多值得擁有這只戒指，她不會因為你把它送給我而生你的氣。好吧，祝你們平安！

（她下，奈莉莎隨後而下。）

安東尼歐（憂傷）：巴薩尼歐大人，給他那只戒指吧。權衡一下你妻子的命令，和他的可敬加上我的愛。

巴薩尼歐（屈服）：去吧，格拉西安諾，快跑追上他。把戒指給他。快去！（格拉西安諾匆忙下。）（對安東尼歐：）來吧，我們去休息。明天一早我們就去貝爾蒙。

（他們一起下。）

（威尼斯法庭外街道；波西亞和奈莉莎上。）

波西亞（把一份文件交給奈莉莎）：問問往猶太人家的路怎麼
　　走。把這給他，叫他簽名。我們今晚就離開，比我們的夫
　　君早一天回到家。羅倫佐會很高興收到這份遺囑。

（格拉西安諾上，因奔跑而喘不過氣。）

格拉西安諾：我終於趕上你們了。巴薩尼歐大人將這只戒指
　　送給你。

波西亞：我滿懷感謝收下他這只戒指，請如此轉告他。還有
　　一件事！請告訴我的書記，老夏洛克家在哪裡。

格拉西安諾：我會的。

奈莉莎（對波西亞）：先生，有話和您說。（她把波西亞拉到一
　　邊。）我來看看能否拿到我丈夫的戒指──那只他發誓會
　　永遠保有的戒指！

波西亞：你可以拿到，我確定。他們無疑地會發誓，他們把戒
　　指送給了男人！但我們會起而面對他們，還要罵得比他們
　　大聲。現在，快去！你知道我會在哪裡等你。

（波西亞下。）

奈莉莎（對格拉西安諾）：來吧，好先生。你可以帶我去他家
　　嗎？

（他們朝夏洛克家的方向離開。）

第五幕

●第一場 ————————————————— P. 111

（羅倫佐與潔西卡在波西亞貝爾蒙住家的花園裡；這是個月光明照的夏夜；波西亞的僕人史迪凡諾跑進來，後面跟著巴薩尼歐的僕人朗西洛特。）

史迪凡諾：哈囉！羅倫佐大人在哪裡？

羅倫佐：別大喊大叫，老兄！我就是。

史迪凡諾：有個信差帶來消息，我的女主人早上就會到達。

朗西洛特：我的主人也在路上了。

（朗西洛特下。）

羅倫佐：親愛的，我們進去為他們的歸來作準備吧。然而，怎麼？我們為什麼要進去？（對史迪凡諾：）我的朋友史迪凡諾，請告訴屋裡的人，你的女主人就快回來了，然後把樂師帶到外面來。（史迪凡諾進屋裡。）照在這裡的月光多麼甜美！我們坐下來，讓樂聲輕柔地落入我們的耳中。看啊，潔西卡，看夜空中滿布著明亮的金色地磚。就連最小的星星移動時，都像合唱團的天使般唱著它的樂章。這樣的和諧也存在不朽的靈魂裡，但當我們還擁有這凡人的驅殼時，我們是聽不到的。（樂師從屋裡出來又消失在樹林裡，羅倫佐對他們大喊。）開始演奏吧。讓柔美的和弦傳入你家女主人的耳中，並以音樂將她帶回家。（對潔西卡：）聽這樂聲吧！

（音樂演奏；波西亞和奈莉莎上。）

波西亞（看著房子）：我們看到的亮光，正是我門廳裡燃燒的燈火。那支小小的蠟燭可以把光亮投射得這麼遠！善行也是這樣照亮邪惡的世界。

奈莉莎：當月亮照耀時，我們就看不到燭火。

波西亞：那是因為更大的力量，會讓較弱者變得暗淡無光。一個替身，在真正的國王走近之前，看起來就像國王一樣莊嚴。國王接近後，他的重要性會變小，就像一條內陸的河川流入大海時一樣。（她傾聽。）有音樂！你聽！

奈莉莎：那是你自己的樂師，從你家裡傳來的音樂。

波西亞：環境真是重要啊！我覺得比白天時聽來還要甜美。

奈莉莎：小姐，是寂靜讓它變好聽了。

波西亞：沒人在聽時，烏鴉的歌聲就像雲雀一樣悅耳。如果夜鶯在白天歌唱，當穀倉裡的家禽都在咯咯叫時，牠還會被認為是比鷦鷯更好的歌手嗎？多少東西在對的季節和對的時刻，會聽來更加美妙！現在，安靜下來！月亮在雲後休息，不想被吵醒呢。

（音樂隨著月光隱去而停了下來。）

羅倫佐：喔，那個聲音——或者我大錯特錯——是波西亞！

波西亞：你認得我的聲音，一如盲人認得杜鵑鳥的聲音——從難聽的聲音得知。

羅倫佐：親愛的小姐，歡迎回家！

波西亞：我們一直在為我們夫君的健康平安而祈禱。他們回來了嗎？

羅倫佐：沒有，小姐，還沒有。但信差說，他們在路上了。

波西亞：進去屋裡，奈莉莎，告訴僕人不要提到我們不在的事，你也不可以，羅倫佐，還有你，潔西卡！

（號角響起，宣告巴薩尼歐到來。）

羅倫佐：你丈夫就快到了。（眨眼。）我們不會告密，小姐，別擔心。

（雲朵飄走，舞台再次沐浴在月光下。）

波西亞：這個夜晚看起來很像生病的白晝。看起來較為蒼白
　　些——就像太陽被遮住的白晝。

（巴薩尼歐、安東尼歐、格拉西安諾和他們的隨從上；格拉西安諾與
　　奈莉莎站在一邊，低聲交談。）

波西亞：歡迎回家，大人。

巴薩尼歐：謝謝你，夫人。也歡迎我的朋友，就是這一位——
　　這是安東尼歐——我虧欠他好多。

波西亞：你應該感到萬分榮幸，我聽說他幾乎為你清償了一
　　大筆債務。

安東尼歐：都是我樂意付出的。

波西亞：我們家非常歡迎你。

格拉西安諾（對奈莉莎，他們為了戒指在爭吵）：明月在上，我發
　　誓你錯怪我了！事實上，我把它給了法官的書記員。因為
　　你這麼在意這件事，我的愛，他就算失去男性雄風，我也
　　不在乎。

波西亞（無意中聽到）：已經吵架了？怎麼回事？

格拉西安諾：是關於一個金戒指，她給我的一個微不足道的
　　戒指。上面刻著字：「愛我，就別離開我。」

奈莉莎：為什麼談上面的字或是它的價值？你發誓會戴著
　　它，直到你臨終的一刻！你說，它會和你一起躺在你的墓
　　穴裡。因為你熱情的誓言，你應該一直保有它。你竟把它
　　給了法官的書記員！我很清楚，那個書記員從來沒有長過
　　鬍子！

格拉西安諾：他會有的，等他長成男人以後。

奈莉莎：是啦，如果女人可以長成男人！

格拉西安諾：喔，以我的榮譽起誓！我把它給了一位年輕人，
　　男孩似的人。個子小小，乾乾淨淨的男孩，不比你高。他請
　　求把它當報酬，我不忍心拒絕他。

波西亞：我得老實說，你該受譴責。這麼輕易就把你妻子的第一件禮物送人！我給了我的愛人一只戒指，並要他發誓絕不與戒指分開，他就站在這裡——我保證他沒有離棄它，或者，就算為了全世界的財富，也沒有把它從手指上拿下來。現在，說真的，格拉西安諾，你已經讓你的妻子傷心了，如果是我，我會為此而發怒。

巴薩尼歐（竊語）：我最好把我的左手砍掉，然後發誓我是為了保護戒指而失去左手。

格拉西安諾：巴薩尼歐大人把他的戒指，送給了向他要求戒指的法官。他也的確配得那只戒指。然後，他的書記員，花了好多功夫處理文件，跟我要我的戒指。不管是書記員還是法官，除了戒指什麼都不要。

波西亞：你把那一只戒指給人了，大人？不是我送你的那一只吧，但願不是。

巴薩尼歐：如果我可以用謊言掩飾過錯，我就會否認。但你可以看到我的手指上並沒有戒指，我失去戒指了。

波西亞（轉過身）：你虛假的心毫無真心誠意！老天在上，在我看到戒指之前，我不會與你同床。

奈莉莎（對格拉西安諾）：我也不會與你同床，格拉西安諾，直到我再次看到我的戒指為止。

巴薩尼歐：親愛的波西亞！如果你知道，我把戒指給了誰、為了誰、以及為了什麼原因，你就不會這麼生氣了！

波西亞：如果你知道這只戒指的意義，或是認清給你戒指的她的一半價值，或是了解你保護它的責任，你絕不會和它分開！沒有人這麼不講理，堅持要一個這麼具有情感價值的東西。奈莉莎的想法是對的，我敢說，的確是某個女人得到了那只戒指！

巴薩尼歐：我以人格擔保，夫人，沒有女人得到它。我把它給了一名法官，他拒絕我的三千金幣，而要求要那只戒指。起初，我拒絕了他——即使他救了我親愛朋友的性命！親愛的夫人，我能說什麼？我不得不追過去把戒指送給他。我滿心羞愧，對他深感失禮，我不想讓我的榮譽因這樣的忘恩負義而被玷污。原諒我，好夫人。滿天星辰在上，如果你在場，我想你也會求我把戒指送給那位可敬的法官。

波西亞：讓那位法官永遠不要靠近我！但既然他得到了我所愛且你發誓會為我保有的珠寶，那麼我要像你一樣大方，我不會拒絕給他任何他所要求的一切——我的身體和我丈夫的床。我將會認識他，我確信。如果我一個人在家，我以名譽擔保——給予是我的權利——我會讓那位法官成為我的床伴！

奈莉莎：而我和他的書記員也是！因此，小心別讓我一個人在家！

格拉西安諾：那麼，你就這麼做吧。但別讓我逮到他，因為如果我逮到他，我就要——

安東尼歐（插話）：我是造成這些爭吵的不愉快主題，真令人傷心。

波西亞：先生，請你別煩惱。不管發生什麼事，我們還是歡迎你的。

巴薩尼歐：波西亞，原諒我這一次過錯，我是被迫的。我們的朋友為證，我向你發誓，我絕不會再違背另一次誓言！

安東尼歐：我曾為了讓他得到幸福而抵押我的身體，但倘若不是這個得到你戒指的人，我已失去了生命。現在，我斗膽再當一次保人，以我的靈魂為賭注，我發誓你的丈夫絕不會再次違背對你立下的誓言。

波西亞：那麼，你將擔任他的保人。（脫下戒指。）把這個給他，告訴他，跟另外那只戒指比，要更加好好保管這只。

安東尼歐：來吧，巴薩尼歐大人。發誓會保管好這只戒指。

巴薩尼歐：蒼天為證，這正是我給法官的那只戒指。

波西亞：我從他那裡拿到的。原諒我，巴薩尼歐。為了回報拿回這只戒指，法官和我上床了。

奈莉莎（也拿出一只戒指）：原諒我，仁慈的格拉西安諾。那個男孩，法官的書記員，昨晚和我上床，以作為這只戒指的報酬。

格拉西安諾：怎麼，我們的妻子在我們應得之前，已經不貞了嗎？

波西亞：別說得那麼粗俗。（她決定解釋。）這裡是一封來自帕多瓦的貝拉利歐的信。你們可以從信裡得知，波西亞就是法官，而奈莉莎是她的書記員。羅倫佐可以證明，我在你走之後不久也離開了，剛剛才回來，還沒進家門呢。安東尼歐，歡迎！我有比你期待更好的消息在等著你。（她拿出另一封信。）請讀這封信。上面說，你有三艘船出乎意料地安全抵達港口。我如何碰巧拿到這封信是個秘密。

安東尼歐：什麼？我說不出話來了！

巴薩尼歐（對波西亞）：你是法官，而我沒有認出你來？

格拉西安諾（對奈莉莎）：你是那個想要背著我搞外遇的書記員？

奈莉莎：是的，但書記員從未打算這麼做──除非他成為一個男人！

巴薩尼歐（對波西亞）：親愛的法官，你將和我上床！而當我不在家，就和我的妻子上床。

安東尼歐（看完他的信後）：親愛的夫人，你給了我生命和未來。因為現在我確定了，我的船隻已安全回港。

波西亞：現在，羅倫佐，我的書記員也有好消息要告訴你。

奈莉莎：我不收分文就給他。（她把已備妥的遺囑交給他。）我在此要把一份來自富有猶太人的契據作為特別禮物交給你和潔西卡，在他死後，你們將得到他所有的財產。

羅倫佐：好夫人，你們把上天所賜的美食，放在即將餓死之人眼前！

波西亞：天快亮了。我相信，你們還不知道全部的經過。我們進屋裡去，你們可以在裡面問問題，而我們會全盤據實以告。

格拉西安諾：就這麼辦。我的奈莉莎要回答的第一個問題是：她寧願等到明天晚上，還是，在離天亮只有兩個小時的現在就上床？如果是白天，我會希望它天黑，如此我得以和法官的書記員上床。在我有生之年，沒有一件事比奈莉莎戒指的安全，更讓我憂心的了！

（眾人手挽著手進屋。）

Literary Glossary ● 文學詞彙表

aside 竊語

一種台詞。演員在台上講此台詞時，其他角色是聽不見的。角色通常藉由竊語來向觀眾抒發內心感受。

■ Although she appeared to be calm, the heroine's **aside** revealed her inner terror.
  雖然女主角看似冷靜，但她的**竊語**透露出她內在的恐懼。

....

backstage 後台

一個戲院空間。演員都在此處準備上台，舞台布景也存放此處。

■ Before entering, the villain impatiently waited **backstage**.
  在上台前，壞人在**後台**焦躁地等待。

....

cast 演員；卡司陣容

戲劇的全體演出人員。

■ The entire **cast** must attend tonight's dress rehearsal.
  全體演員必須參加今晚的正式排練。

....

character 角色

故事或戲劇中虛構的人物。

■ Mighty Mouse is one of my favorite cartoon **characters**.
  太空飛鼠是我最愛的卡通**人物**之一。

....

climax 劇情高峰

戲劇或小說中主要衝突的結局。

■ The outlaw's capture made an exciting **climax** to the story.
  逃犯落網成為故事中最刺激的**精彩情節**。

....

comedy 喜劇

有趣好笑的戲劇、電影和電視劇，並有快樂完美的結局。

- My friends and I always enjoy a Jim Carrey **comedy**.
  我朋友和我總是很喜歡金凱瑞演的**喜劇**。

---

conflict 戲劇衝突

故事主要的角色較量、勢力對抗或想法衝突。

- *Dr. Jekyll and Mr. Hyde* illustrates the **conflict** between good and evil.
  《變身怪醫》描述善惡之間的**衝突**。

---

conclusion 尾聲；結局

解決情節衝突的方法，使故事結束。

- That play's **conclusion** was very satisfying. Every conflict was resolved. 該劇的**結局**十分令人滿意，所有的衝突都被圓滿解決。

---

dialogue 對白

小說或戲劇角色所說的話語。

- Amusing **dialogue** is an important element of most comedies.
  有趣的**對白**是大多喜劇中重要的元素之一。

---

drama 戲劇

故事，通常非喜劇類型，特別是寫來讓演員在戲劇或電影中演出。

- The TV **drama** about spies was very suspenseful.
  那齣關於間諜的電視**劇**非常懸疑。

---

event 事件

發生的事情；特別的事。

- The most exciting **event** in the story was the surprise ending.
  故事中最精彩的**事件**是意外的結局。

---

introduction 簡介

一篇簡短的文章，呈現並解釋小說或戲劇的劇情。

■ The **introduction** to *Frankenstein* is in the form of a letter.
《科學怪人》的**簡介**是以信件的形式呈現。

....

motive 動機

一股內在或外在的力量，迫使角色做出某些事情。

■ What was that character's **motive** for telling a lie?
那個角色說謊的**動機**為何？

....

passage 段落

書寫作品的部分內容，範圍短至一行，長至幾段。

■ His favorite **passage** from the book described the author's childhood.
他在書中最喜歡的**段落**描述了該作者的童年。

....

playwright 劇作家

戲劇的作者。

■ William Shakespeare is the world's most famous **playwright**.
威廉莎士比亞是世界上最知名的**劇作家**。

....

plot 情節

故事或戲劇中一連串的因果事件，導致最終結局。

■ The **plot** of that mystery story is filled with action.
該推理故事的**情節**充滿打鬥。

....

point of view 觀點

由角色的心理層面來看待故事發展的狀況。

■ The father's **point of view** about elopement was quite different from the daughter's. 父親對於私奔的**看法**與女兒迥然不同。

....

prologue 序幕

在戲劇第一幕開始前的介紹。

- The playwright described the main characters in the **prologue** to the play.

  劇作家在**序幕**中描述了主要角色。

---

quotation 名句

被引述的文句；某角色所説的詞語；在引號內的文字。

- A popular **quotation** from *Julius Caesar* begins, "Friends, Romans, countrymen . . ."

  《凱撒大帝》中**常被引用的文句**開頭是：「各位朋友，各位羅馬人，各位同胞……」。

---

role 角色

演員在劇中揣摩表演的人物。

- Who would you like to see play the **role** of Romeo?

  你想看誰飾演羅密歐這個**角色**呢？

---

sequence 順序

故事或事件發生的時序。

- Sometimes actors rehearse their scenes out of **sequence**.

  演員有時會不按**順序**排練他們出場的戲。

---

setting 情節背景

故事發生的地點與時間。

- This play's **setting** is New York in the 1940s.

  戲劇的**背景設定**於 1940 年代的紐約。

---

soliloquy 獨白

角色向觀眾發表想法的一番言論，猶如自言自語。

- One famous **soliloquy** is Hamlet's speech that begins, "To be, or not to be …"
  哈姆雷特最知名的**獨白**是：「生，抑或是死……」。

---

symbol 象徵

用以代表其他事物的人或物。

- In Hawthorne's famous novel, the scarlet letter is a **symbol** for adultery.
  在霍桑知名的小說中，紅字是姦淫罪的**象徵**。

---

theme 主題

戲劇或小說的主要意義；中心思想。

- Ambition and revenge are common **themes** in Shakespeare's plays.
  在莎士比亞的劇作中，野心與報復是常見的**主題**。

---

tragedy 悲劇

嚴肅且有悲傷結局的戲劇。

- *Macbeth*, the shortest of Shakespeare's plays, is a **tragedy**.
  莎士比亞最短的劇作《馬克白》是部**悲劇**。
